# *Thirst for You*

## ISLAND EMBERS, Book 3

*Welcome to Quiet Whisper*

# CHERYL BARTON

About the *Island Embers* Series:

Join me on this journey into a new sexy, romantic series called, Island Embers. How, do you ask, would embers be used to describe something like a budding romance when its definition means something that's burning away, fading even? Well, that's true, but in this series, embers signify a place where love and desire, which could be fading, flourish again as the embers are ignited hotter and fiercer than ever.

In this series of three books, *Hunger for You*, *Desire for You* and *Thirst for You*, three brothers, Tellum, Byrum and Callum Blackstone have enjoyed their lives as bachelors, never thinking that there would be a woman for each of them who could stoke the desires of their hearts as they do their bodies.

In the business of building romantic resorts, *Secret Whisper*, *Silent Whisper*, and *Quiet Whisper*, each brother will discover that the heart wants what it wants. Their lives are no longer only about intoxicating, lust-filled needs. The grown and sexy in them have found it's about everlasting love.

Thanks for joining me in this third and final helping of the series with, *Thirst for You*. This is Callum Blackstone's path to forever.

About – *Thirst for You: Quiet Whisper, Book 3*

Callum Blackstone did the unforgiveable. He was caught with his ex-girlfriend by his then girlfriend, Kendra Grimes. A year after their relationship ended, Kendra showed up asking for help for their twin boys that he didn't know he had. Putting their issues aside, they focus on getting their sons the medical help they need.

As they began to heal, Callum knew that in order to get Kendra back in his life so that he could be a full-time father to his sons, he had to work on a secret, quiet plan of love, adoration and untamed lust to get her to trust him again.

There was no better place to do that than on the island of Hawaii at his new resort, *Quiet Whisper*. It was a magical place that anything wished for could be made true. He was counting on everlasting love being the end result. Winning over Kendra's heart again wouldn't be easy. After leaving him once, love is what he hoped would bring her back to him in one of the most beautiful places in the world. He was up for the challenge because his thirst for her has never quenched.

***Welcome to Quiet Whisper!***

## Dedication

To the lovers of all things love and romance, I salute you. As a writer, I appreciate you. As a reader, I understand your desire for more love! I dedicate this sexy love story to you. May you continue to read and allow the words within this book to take your mind away to someplace happy and healthy where love and romance resides. Thanks for staying on this love train with me.


*Cheryl*

# From the Ending of *Desire for You*
## Book 2 of the Island Embers series

## *From Silent Whisper to Quiet Whisper in Honolulu, Hawaii*

Byrum waved Tellum and Cheyenne over to the seats he held for them in order to enjoy a battle of the bands concert that was being hosted at *Silent Whisper*. A month after the grand opening, the resort was full with excitement for the event. Keiko tapped his shoulder so that he would change seats with her, allowing her the chance to sit next to Cheyenne. Where they could have sat in VIP seating, Byrum wanted them to experience the concert from the vantage point of their general stay guests. They were minutes from the lights going down as the event host made her way to the stage to get things started.

"Where's Callum?" Byrum asked Tellum when he and Cheyenne took their seats.

"He's at *Quiet Whisper*. He was planning to join us but he had some friends who were coming to the island to hang out with him for a few days. You know what it's like when Lucas finds time to get away from touring to catch up with him. I told him I would let you know that he wasn't coming," Tellum said.

Byrum leaned over and hugged Cheyenne after she and Keiko greeted each other.

"Can I?" Byrum asked Cheyenne pointing.

"Of course. Uncles and godfathers are always welcome. I can't wait for y'all to meet this little lady," she said before he reached out and placed his hand over her growing belly.

"How far along are you?" Keiko asked.

"I'm officially six months as of yesterday."

"Are you ready to be a father, Tellum?" Byrum asked him once they'd all settled in.

"Man, this is the longest nine-months in the world. I'm more than ready. After her miscarriage, we're excited that there are no issues this time. That was a hard time for us all. That only made me want to be a father even more. I'm already making plans to get baby number two in the making before this one is a year old," he joked.

"Don't listen to your brother. When he's had night after night of not sleeping, feedings and diaper changes, he won't be so excited about another one so soon," Cheyenne kidded.

"How is Tru?" Cheyenne asked Keiko. "I may need to all you with some motherly advice."

"Call me anytime you want. Tru is doing good. He's actually with my parents in Boston while I'm here for this week with Byrum. No longer living on the island full time is an adjustment. I think Tru is more upset than I am. He went to school here until December and loved it. He wasn't ready to go back to Detroit. I reminded him that we would travel back and forth. He was supposed to be with his father, but he is on a trip with his new girlfriend."

"Tru is getting tall. Before we left to come back here, I had to raise the seat on his bicycle because his legs are getting longer," Byrum added.

"I guess mom actually got a grandchild even before Cheyenne got pregnant by way of Tru. I called her a few weeks ago from *Secret Whisper* and Tru was spending the night with her and Pop. That had to be fun," Tellum said.

"Bro, when I tell you that mom loves him as if he was her actual grandson, I mean that. She gets excited when she gets to spend time with him. Out of the blue when we stopped by for a visit and Tru was with us, we were talking about a movie Keiko and I wanted to go see. She told us to go. She would keep Tru. That turned into him having so much fun with them that he asked to spend the night. Dad even ran to the store to grab him some pajamas and other stuff he would need so that Keiko wouldn't have to go back to our place to get him a change of clothes. At least we get to see first-hand how good they're going to be with your new bundle after Cheyenne gives birth," Byrum said.

"That's the truth," Tellum acknowledged. "She is a big help to Cheyenne now. Life is good?" he asked Byrum.

"Damn right it is!" Byrum shouted as heads turned to look in his direction. When people saw who he was, the berating that they would have given someone else turned into cute waves of hello.

The lights in the concert arena went down, signaling the start of the show. Byrum knew they would finish catching up at dinner after the show which was already planned out.

Before he could get comfortable to enjoy the evening, Byrum's phone vibrated in his pocket. Keiko looked at him to signal that if it's work-related, he should ignore it.

"Baby, it's Callum. He said he needed to speak to me and Tellum, right now. There were about thirty exclamation points added to the end of the text."

"Yeah, I got the same text. Bro, let's step out. He knows we're at the concert. It's eight in the morning there in Hawaii. It must be important. We'll be right back," Tellum said.

Byrum followed him out into the main lobby.

"I wonder what this is about?" Byrum asked opening up the video chat app to talk with Callum. His brother answered on the first ring.

To say that Callum looked ragged would be an understatement. He looked like he was carrying the weight of the world on his shoulders.

"Bro, what's going on? Why the urgency?" Tellum asked.

Byrum looked closer into the screen.

"Are you at a hospital? It looks like a hospital lobby behind you. What the hell is going on?"

"I need you and Tellum to meet me here in Hawaii as soon as you can. I wouldn't usually ask you to uproot your lives and hop on a plane, but I need you here. Pop is already on his way from Detroit," Callum pleaded.

Byrum and Tellum both heard and saw the urgency. They were concerned that Callum had another drinking binge, which he promised them that he would stop doing after the incident with his ex, Kendra over a year ago.

"Callum, tell us what's going on. Are you hurt? Did something happen to someone on the construction site at the resort? Talk to us," Tellum said.

"Nothing like that. Kendra arrived here today," Callum explained.

"Okay. Is she okay?" Byrum asked.

"She is but my sons aren't," Callum explained.

Tellum and Byrum looked to each other and mouthed the word, sons.

"Callum, what are you talking about? Sons? You don't have any sons. Have you been drinking?" Byrum questioned.

"Let me start over. When Kendra and I broke up a little over a year ago, I didn't know she was pregnant. She didn't know either," Callum started to explain further.

"When did you find out?" Tellum asked.

"A few hours ago. She called me last night and asked if I was in Detroit. I told her I was here in Hawaii with some friends. She asked if she could come here to talk to me. Of course, I agreed. I haven't spoken to her since she broke up with me. I tried for over six-months with no response from her at all. I didn't know she was pregnant. When she landed at the airport, I met her there. You know I was shocked to see her with two babies along with her mother and sister. She ran everything down to me."

"What? That she had two whole ass babies and never told you? Never told this family? Who does that?" Tellum asked.

"You'd be surprised how pissed off a woman can actually be," Byrum said.

"True, and she was. The issue is, both boys are sick. They are almost four months old and have diagnosed congenital heart defects. They have complex valve or heart rhythm disorders. They're going to need surgeries. As their father, I'm going to give blood for the surgeries they'll need. You should see them all tiny and sick. They have feeding and breathing issues, among other things. You should see them. They look just like me, before you ask."

"Neither of us were going to ask that. If you already know, that's all we need to hear. Callum, you had that problem as a baby. Do you remember mom telling us the story of how you made it through that touch and go time in your life?"

"I know. I told Kendra that. I'm scared for them. Pop just called and said he talked with some friends of his in the medical field who put him in touch with a Dr. Clayton Myers out of Texas. The doctor told him to get the twins to Texas Children's Hospital as soon as possible. When he told him the babies were here in Hawaii, he patched Pop in to a doctor from that hospital who said before we put them on another flight, he wanted to check them over. Dr. Myers is on his way here to Hawaii along with his wife who is also a doctor. We'll then get the babies to Texas for care if need be. He believes they can get the care here considering who we are. He knows that we can afford to bring in any doctor from anywhere in the world that we need."

"Kendra flew them all the way to Hawaii?" Tellum asked.

"She was scared and didn't trust anyone. She said the doctor who was treating them in Las Vegas wasn't as forthcoming as she thought he should be. Even though the issue was diagnosed, she felt like they were using the boys' condition for research. That frightened her. Her team coach helped her get a medical flight to Hawaii after she told her that I was here and she needed to get them to their father; the only man she trusted to help her look after their care. She looks like she hasn't slept in months. Not just because she has twins but because of worry. Look, I know I'm asking a lot, but can you get here for support? I really need my brothers; I need my family."

"How are they right now?" Byrum asked.

"They were given strict instructions for the boys from Dr. Myers. I was finally able to convince Kendra and her family to get some sleep. It took a lot to get them to leave the hospital. I promised her that I would not leave their side until she got back. They're staying in a part of *Silent Whisper* that is already complete. I was going to do a hotel but I figured they would get more rest there because there is only staff on the premises who promised me that they would look after Kendra and her family as if they were their own family. Look, can you get here?"

Tellum stepped away and pulled out his phone.

"We're calling the airport right now. As soon as the jet can get us there, you'll see us. Hold it together. If a doctor is flying out, I'm sure he's the best. Tell Kendra we're on our way."

"I'll see you when you get here. I've got sons. Can you believe that?"

"I can. You loved that girl or there wouldn't be any babies," Byrum said.

"As quiet as it's kept, I've always and only loved Kendra. She'll never believe that. Our kids brought us back together. I'm never letting go; not ever," Callum declared.

"I'm happy to hear that, but don't forget what you did to

make her leave you. I don't think she'll forget even with the boys being sick. What are their names?" Byrum asked.

"Finn and Liam. They don't have my last name, but they will. The only thing that matters right now is getting them healthy."

"Bro, you overcame the same defect and so will they. I need to go and make Cheyenne and Keiko aware that we need to get to Hawaii. We'll take my jet and leave Tellum's here for them to return home to Detroit. Hold on. We're on our way. Our phones are on or call the phone in the jet. If we need to get anything and everyone there to care for our nephews, a simple text will do."

"I love them, Byrum. I love my boys and I just met them."

"And Kendra?"

"I have to find a way to make up what I did to hurt her. I can't have my boys getting healthy and she walks back out of my life. I have them; I still want her. That thirst I once told you I had for her that could never be quenched by another woman? It's true. I didn't realize it until I saw her in a helpless state. Then I saw my boys and knew that I messed our lives up by being messy. I'm putting all that behind me. My focus has to be on my life with my sons and if Kendra could ever forgive me, my life with her."

"Bro, don't worry. That thirst you've always had for Kendra won't go away. I believe it will be a part of what brings you back together. If you want her, you fight for her. Just like we want Finn and Liam to fight to stay here with us, with this family, have that same fight in you to win your family. There is no better place to do that than at *Quiet Whisper*. We're on our way," Byrum said.

The call ended at the same time that Tellum's did with their pilot.

"We ready?" Tellum asked.

"Let's roll. A Blackstone is in trouble. We ride before dawn!" they said together as they sprinted back inside to alert their women.

**

Callum went back into the hospital room where his sons were hooked up to so many machines with wires everywhere that he couldn't stop the tears that rolled down his face even if he tried.

"Daddy is here. I'm never leaving you," he said.

"Are you?"

Callum turned and his eyes met Kendra's.

"You're back already?" he asked.

"Are you?" she asked.

"Am I what?"

"Are you here for them? I mean, not just because they're sick."

"I am here for them now that I know about them. I'm here for you too."

"Callum, I don't need you to be here for me. I need you to be here for our sons. There is no you and I anymore. I hope you get that. We are one when it comes to them. As for us, nothing has changed."

Before he could answer, Kendra stepped away when a nurse walked by. He turned his attention back to his sons. He leaned close to them where they laid in a clear glass hospital cradle together.

"We will be a family and that includes your mother. I knew it the minute she got off the plane with the two of you. I messed up not realizing what I had with her. I promise you that I will fight with everything in me to get her back. I thirst for her. I always have and I always will. You have to get better so that you can help me convince her that I'm not that Callum anymore. In fact, I'm the Callum who has two sons. Fight to stay here with us and I promise you that I will fight to get our family together."

Before he could say another word, signals and sirens around the boys began to go off as doctors and nurses raced into the room. He cried when they asked him to step out of the room where he found Kendra shaking uncontrollably in the doorway. He pulled her away with him and held her tight. Thankfully, she didn't fight him. They needed to reserve their energy to fight for the lives of their sons. At the same time, he was also fighting for him and her.

As more medical staff raced into the room, Callum hoped his family could get to Hawaii and do it fast. He and Kendra needed them. The real revelation was, he now knew how much he has always wanted, needed and desired Kendra; only her. Now was the time that he got serious about life and love and faced his real truth. His life hasn't been the same since she left him. His goal now is to prove to her that they could have forever if only she could forgive him.

# 1

*One year ago – Chicago, Illinois*

In the midst of the vivid Chicago night life of spectacular clubs, packed and lively bars, breweries that shelled out the best alcohol and even casinos, with two being owned and operated by two men he considered close friends and allies in the business world, one of those casinos is where Callum Blackstone found himself having the best night of his life. Nothing and no one could steal the pleasantries that he was experiencing during this much-needed downtime. He was the party king of the Blackstone family. Being from Detroit, he was no stranger to amazing and energetic casinos. There were several in Detroit that he frequented and got his life on.

His love for all things Las Vegas, especially their casinos also was not foreign to him. He was able to spend some extra time there since that's where his current love interest, Kendra Grimes lived and made a living as a basketball player. She was a star guard for the Las Vegas WNBA basketball team. He'd actually met her a few years ago. They have been in an on-again, off-again type relationship for most of that time. Currently, they were semi-on with things, but with her travel schedule with the team and his successful business of resort development, restoration and building, he was also away just as she was. Making a steady relationship work was a problem. Hence one of the reasons he was in Chicago. The invite was extended and he accepted, mainly because he had time on his hands. He wanted to spend it with Kendra, but she was locked, loaded and too busy for him. His thinking was, when the cats away – and all that good stuff. His roving eye could help him get into something. With social media all over place with his every move being recorded by someone, he learned how to not display what he did on his playing field with anyone who could then get it back to her. He has never been known as the faithful guy in town; definitely not in a party town like Chicago.

Horace Grant, the casino owner reached out and invited him to check the place out. He and his business partner, Torrence Allen had recently opened their second casino in Chicago. They had recently begun to restore their Las Vegas location as well.

Callum's original plan was to take in a show at the Vegas location so that he could also spend some time with Kendra. With all of her complaining about his lack of time for her, he had been trying to do that when she busted up their plans for something else. What? He didn't know. He was too pissed that she had, once again, blown him off. He had hoped that she would understand what his life was like if he and his brothers were to continue making waves in the business world. Their most profitable ventures, so far, had been the creation of three resorts for adults only, though the Hawaii location would have two separate, yet combined resorts. One for adults only and one that was family-oriented. The two options at the same resort would be a one-of-a-kind experience.

The brothers had decided that each of them would take one location and focus on that one by putting their own touches on each location. Tellum's baby was *Secret Whisper,* which was located in Punta Cana in The Dominican Republic. That resort was open and already booked and busy for the next few years with guests who paid in advance so that they were guaranteed a reservation.

Byrum lent his talent to *Silent Whisper*, which was on a private island in the Mediterranean. That resort was also now up and running after a lot of hard work for all three of them, especially Byrum.

Callum beamed with pride that he couldn't wait to celebrate *Quiet Whisper*, the resort he was building in Honolulu, Hawaii. That location was already a tourist attraction. With the addition of his resort, vacationers and loads of money being poured into Hawaii would allow it to continue to flourish. Preliminary work was done, including the purchase of some additional property surrounding what they had already purchased. With the new purchase, they would be able to have direct beach-front, private access for both the adult only and the family fun resorts. With their family growing now that Cheyenne was pregnant and Byrum had fallen in love with his executive assistant, Keiko who came with a son, Tru, they were all beginning to realize that they wanted to expand their thinking beyond what it's like to be a single bachelor to thinking more about getaway spots that were inclusive of family, especially kids. That is what led to them investing more of their money into *Quiet Whisper* than they did at *Secret Whisper* and *Silent Whisper*. Callum knew his work was cut out for him to now spend his time matching and trying to out create both of his older brothers with his ideas for the new resort.

He and his brothers are not strangers to Hawaii. His mother's family was from there. As kids, the family would spend weeks there every summer and sometimes over the Christmas break from school. Now that they were adults, their mother thought that the desire to go to Hawaii to visit family would have ended when they were kids. To them, Hawaii was just as much home for them as was Detroit, which is where they all have made their home fronts.

Like Tellum and Byrum did by living part-time on their resort islands during construction, he would do the same by staying in Hawaii for the foreseeable future. That's why he decided to give himself one last big shebang before diving head first into all the work that was ahead of him.

Like them, he had to hire a lot of staff to help pull it all together. First, he pulled from his team from the Detroit main office of Blackstone Real Estate Investment Trust Corporation, the firm he and his brothers successfully ran. With the help of their father, Dennis Blackstone, who had retired and happily joined them in business as a business consultant, their dreams could only go up from here. With his many years at *General Motors* in Detroit, his father brought a wealth of talent and information that was taking, what is now the family business, to a new level business-wise, in the world, especially financially.

Getting his last moments of fun in without having to consider work for at least the next week, Callum thought that it was the perfect time to get in a little relaxation with friends. On his trek to Chicago, he invited his best friend from Detroit, Lucas Jackson to hang out with him. They grew up together and had been like brothers since they were kids. When Lucas went into the music industry, signing with one of the largest record labels in the country, Callum had turned his attention to college with a focus on business acquisitions. Both paths had provided quite for each of them.

Lucas had a few days off from his world tour where he was drawing hundreds of thousands of fans. He was the perfect choice to join him since Horace and Torrence were interested in Lucas doing a short residency at either of their Chicago casino locations. He already knew that Lucas would do him a solid out of friendship and take them up on the offer.

So far, their time in Chicago was filled with five-star treatment from their rooms, to the food, the transportation around town to the VIP treatment everywhere they went. Most of all, there were women. There were tons of them everywhere. From what he could see, the fun was going to be plentiful, perhaps event at the level that this visit would go down in the history books for him and a great time in life.

Tonight, they had just come from a concert starring the soulful songstress, Victoria Monet, one of his favorites. She was not only beautiful, but could sing any other artist under the table. The concert had been at the first Chicago casino location. They were now at the second, the one that Horace oversaw, after moving from Las Vegas to Chicago to do amazing work; which he did. They were all enjoying themselves at the nightclub in the heart of the casino. The place was packed to the max where his eyes took in one beautiful woman after another. The way they were checking him out, something he was used to, he would have his pick of the tonight. He had locked eyes with several of them within minutes of walking in the door. Music had the place jumping. Celebrities kept the crowd large. After one too many drinks, he began accepting sexy looks and conversations from one luscious looking woman after another.

No doubt, he and his brothers were not just big in the world of business, but they were also social media famous because they each had their own social media handler who kept track of their images and conversations about them on the internet. Having a few million followers was boding well for them when it came to interest in their resorts. More than a few times tonight, Sasha, the woman who oversaw and controlled his social media accounts had messaged him to let him know that there was a lot of talk, video and images of him in Chicago living it up. She recommended that for image-sake, he should pull his fun back just a little bit. Of course, being young, free and the bachelor of all bachelors, he ignored her and continued his night. When Sasha mentioned all the women he was cozying up to that she kept up with when people tagged him in their videos and photos while at the casino, she asked him if he was thinking about Kendra when he carried on with his flirting. He brushed it off and reminded her that he left his mother at home. He wasn't actually talking about his mother, but was, instead, talking about Kendra. He was tired of people, especially women, coming up to him over the past few days inquiring as to whether Kendra was with him. Though he knew that she may have thought that she was the only one for him, he wasn't quite ready to be that kept under lock and key in a relationship. One day he would. Today was not that day.

"Bro, guess what?" Lucas asked walking up to him where he was talking to a woman whose breasts he couldn't take his eyes off of. He was absolutely a breast man. He loved them large and natural. He wasn't a fan of women who altered their bodies unless it was for a medical reason. Just to draw attention, he wasn't a fan of that. This woman's mounds were peeking out and practically screaming at him to have a closer look and touch. He was down for that. He hadn't seen Kendra in three weeks. He was certainly no choir boy. He'd strayed a time or two. It wasn't about the distance. It was about him seeing all that was out here that he wanted to enjoy before he decided to settle down. He had years before he would do that. Again, he thought, today was not that day.

When Lucas shoved him on the arm again, Callum finally stood to his full six-foot-six height from whispering in the ear of the woman who had just offered him the time of his life tonight. He was seconds from taking her up on said offer.

"Luke, really? You can't see that I'm a little preoccupied at the moment. I'm hoping to be quite knee deep or should I say face full in wondering how far down the rabbit hole does her cleavage go. Don't block tonight. What's up?" he said, telling the woman that he would look for her in a bit. From her too tight shorts, sexy high heels and body to die for, he didn't want to know more, he simply wanted to see more. This was his time and he was going to enjoy it.

"I asked you a question. Guess who's here?" Lucas asked again.

"Okay, I'll bite. Is it the princess of thieves? I don't know, fool. Just tell me," Callum quipped.

"Tessa. Your ex is in the building tonight."

Callum looked around.

"Really?"

"Yeah. She probably heard, like the rest of the world did on social media, that you were here tonight."

Callum flipped him off as they often did with each other.

"No, they probably heard that you were here tonight and that *I* was with you. Either way, I had no doubt word would get out. The ratio in this place is three-to-one. I want to take advantage of having my share of three women," Callum gloated.

"All at once?" Lucas joked, and gave him a strong pat on the back. "I'm trying to be like you," he added.

"Don't act like I'm the only one of the two of us who has had a threesome or a foursome before. I'm not talking about doing that tonight, but a few one at a time opportunities before I leave would be nice."

"And Kendra?"

Callum turned full around to Lucas and yelled at him above the music.

"Why is everyone asked me about Kendra tonight? She isn't

here. She is somewhere doing her own thing. We are not glued at the hip. I'm also not a monk, though she's trying to turn me into one by playing the absent game these days. Besides, you know I'm very discreet about mine, just like you are. The R&B superstar that you are, you must know what I'm talking about. How many times have you slipped and landed inside of some sweet, sexy..."

"Don't finish that statement," Lucas said, putting up his hands in surrender.

"I was going to say, sweet, sexy thang, but yeah, that too."

Callum was about to say the word to get his point across. He just wanted to have fun.

"Sure you were. I get what you're saying though."

"Then you get it. Look, I care about Kendra. On some level, I do love her. Right now, we're doing our own career things. She's a professional ballplayer and at the top of her game on a winning team. I make time for her and she makes time for me. We're involved but we never claimed exclusivity. I'm not trying to hurt her, hence, I'm good with what I do behind closed doors."

"Well, what you used to do and who you used to do behind closed doors is coming this way."

Callum turned around as Lucas signaled for his security to let Tessa and her crew of lovely ladies behind the tall, muscular wall of security that surrounded them. Once they let her pass, Tessa walked right up to him. She did what she usually did when they came face to face; she licked her full luscious lips letting him immediately know what she wanted.  Everything about her reminded him of the singer, SZA, with her gorgeous lips and banging body. Where SZA had talent that was off the charts in music and acting, Tessa's only talent was how she used her body to get what she wanted from men. He was once one of those men. The difference in him and other men was that she wanted what he could do to her body. He never sponsored women financially. That wasn't his thing. If he was looking for more than just a good night of wild sex from a woman, he needed her to have more drive than just spreading her legs. Those were the women men played with, but didn't take seriously. He didn't mind his time with Tessa, which had been well-spent before because the things she could do with hers was mysteriously hot and often defying gravity. She was a part of his playground, but not the home team.

They had once been involved, but not seriously enough for them to claim one another. They were having fun and when he went to red carpet events, he sometimes took her as his plus one. He moved on from her the moment he saw and then met Kendra. No woman could match her statuesque stance and beauty. She was five-foot-ten of curved deliciousness. Her body was killer perfect and natural. She was brilliant after graduating both high school and college a few years ahead of others her age. Kendra was the perfect example of the perfect package when he would one day be ready for that. Meeting her after one of her games had been one of his best memories in meeting a woman. She had also been the first that he didn't lead off with getting her between the sheets. They enjoyed hours and hours of talking. He took the time to get to know more than just what he could see. For him, Tessa was all about what he could see. Tonight, he saw all that she had on display.

"Look who is here looking all debonair and sexy as *hell*," Tessa said, almost on a purr like a sexy kitten.

Callum allowed his eyes to travel up and down her body luscious. There were times when he played all around every part of her. He was remembering the many times he'd tasted every part of her from her head to her sexy feet. The way she was looking tonight, he wouldn't mind a stroll up, down and into memory lane.

"If it isn't the ever-so sexy, Tessa Goodhall. How have you been?" he asked, making sure he provided her with a lick of his own lips as his eyes roamed all over her.

Tessa visibly shivered to get all of his attention.

"Better now that I'm getting my fill of those magnetic gray eyes of yours. Your deep, husky voice still makes me shiver, quiver and everything in between when I hear it. I can't help myself. Here alone?" she asked looking around, no doubt in search of Kendra like everyone else had been doing all night.

Callum looked to her friends whom he had yet spoken to. One of them was trying to get Lucas' attention. He laughed when his friend showed no interest. He remembered Tessa's two best friends by sight but not by name. They were cool, but definitely not Lucas' type. His friend loved sexy Black women, as did he. Tessa's friends were not that.

"Ladies? How have you been? Long time, no see," he said, acknowledging them with a distant hug when they each leaned in.

"Good," both ladies said together.

"Now that we've all been greeted and everything, can you focus on me now?" Tessa asked, stepping in the space between him and her friends.

Callum laughed to himself at her boldness.

When her eyes went from her friends and back to him, her girls got the message. In the next second, they excused themselves, leaving him and Tessa alone.

"Do they do tricks as well?" he asked when they took Tessa's signal and walked away without her having to say even one word to them.

"Not the kind of tricks that I can, if you remember. I know it's been a while because you've been all over Kendra or rather, she's always all over you. I guess she wants every woman to know that you belong to her."

Callum shook his head from side to side as his eyes landed on her lips. They were outlined in a darker color than her shining, touch of burgundy lip stick. If he didn't remember anything about her, it was her lips and what they could do to his body. Even now, he was rising to the occasion wondering if they were still just as good, especially to him, as they had been.

"Oh, I remember. Never doubt how unforgettable you are. As for anyone else, if they're not right here in front of me, with me or around me in this very spot, they don't matter."

"Really? You haven't forgotten about me? If that's the case, how come I haven't heard from you since you hooked up with Kendra?"

"You know how it is."

"Oh, I know. You dropped me like a hot potato for her. I get it. She's stunningly beautiful. I respect your attraction to her and that killer body. She's also smart. She comes from a famous family with her father being a former NBA star who now coaches the number one NBA team in the country. I get it. Top-tier is drawn to top-tier. We could have still been having some side fun. Do you have plans for tonight? I'm thinking maybe I could invite you to my room for a cup of coffee; or *not*. I'm staying here in the casino on the fourth floor. No doubt you're in one of the presidential suites on the top floor."

"That I am," he said.

Tessa leaned closer to him until she was a whisper away from his lips before going around close to his ear. He leaned down so that he could hear her better.

"I've never stopped craving that part of you that is bigger, better, gets harder and gets the job done better than any man I've ever known. I can keep a secret if you let me have a taste to remember old, delicious times. One more time for old times' sake?"

If Tessa was ever anything at all, it wasn't shy. She never had a problem in expressing herself or being blunt about what she wanted. Callum didn't immediately respond. They locked eyes and stayed that way as images of what they could be doing was going around in both of their heads. No one would know. He could slip out of the club and no one would ever suspect.

He thought about the repercussions of getting involved with Tessa again even for one night. He knew he could do it and get back to his life. He didn't know if it was the alcohol or lust that had him thinking about taking her up on her offer.

"One time?" he asked.

The moment she knew what he was talking about, Tessa leaned back and laughed out loud, pressing one brightly manicured hand to his chest.

"Right. You are not a one-round kind of brother. *Mmm*, I love that about you. Let me clarify then. This one night will be for however many rounds you are up for."

Her eyes cascaded down his body. He allowed his eyes to follow where hers landed.

"Tessa, you're in your mischievous phase," he noted.

"Looks to me like your body is doing the most talking. You look ready for round one right now. I have an itch," she slurred out.

"I know what your itches are like."

"Then meet me in my room."

She whispered her room number to him and walked toward the exit of the club. Just then Lucas walked back up.

"Bro, you're doing it? Or should I say, doing her?"

Callum placed his beer bottle on the closest table.

"Damn, right I am. I'll catch you later."

"Don't do it. That spider web looks like it will be full with all kinds of regret for you. You know she came here specifically for you. These women cannot be trusted. She knows you're with Kendra, yet here she is."

"Lighten up, Luke. I'll get in and out before I'm even missed. I'll make my way back down here. If not, I'll catch you in the morning. That web can snare a brother like you wouldn't believe. I need a little release. Hold things down here. If Horace comes looking for me, tell him I decided to make it a short night. I'll catch him before I head back to Detroit. I then have a flight to Hawaii in two days. Are you good if I head out?"

"I am. Your security guy took a break with one of my guys."

Callum almost forgot that he had one of the men he often took with him as his security for the night.

"When Jesse gets back, tell him he can take off. I won't need him for the rest of my time here. He's got family here that he wanted to spend time with. He could use the time off."

"Is he traveling with you to Hawaii?" Lucas inquired.

"No. I don't take security with me when I go there. That place is like being at home. I do have a few guys in Hawaii that I contract with for security if I need it. The resort is off limits to guests and my family who live there, most who look like sumo wrestlers, always have my back."

"Ah, you're taking about Chief."

"Yeah, we call him that, though is name is Mana. He's close in age to me and my brothers. When I'm in Hawaii, he's got me covered. Hold down the fort?"

"You know it. In fact, this woman I was just talking to is a prospect for keeping me company on the dance floor. Be careful with Tessa."

"I hear you. She's harmless. Sexy as ever, but definitely harmless."

Callum turned and walked toward the exit that led to the elevator to the casino hotel rooms. He didn't see Tessa but assumed she was on her way to her rom. He moved to the side and stood to give her a few extra minutes to be there before him. He didn't want a lot of pre-sex stuff going on. He was all about the fun and so was she; that much he remembered.

Before he moved, he patted his pocket to remind himself that he was glad he remembered to bring protection along. That was important to him. He loved his fun but he never had any without it. His one exception had been Kendra. If he were paying attention, he would have seen Tessa huddled off to the side with her friends.

Callum didn't know that a slight oversight, like not paying attention, would cost him dearly.

**

"You're sure you saw her here?" Tessa asked Ellie and Cate, her two best friends who flew in with her from Florida where they lived.

Two days ago, Callum's face had been all over social media showing him in Chicago. She quickly pulled together a plan that would have her front and center with him. Unexpected guests was the best part that she hadn't planned for but very much loved.

Ellie pointed and Tessa followed with her eyes. Entering the club was Kendra, Callum's girlfriend. Even though she didn't know Kendra, she hated her. She had taken Callum away. He had been her ticket to the high-life that now escaped her. Sure, she had the body and know-how to attract well-to-do men. The one she wanted, was Callum. She hated that he merely saw her as a play thing and not girlfriend potential like Kendra. See her walk into the club tonight, she now had a new plan.

"She just missed Callum. He went out the other entrance,"

Cate said.

"Good. I have to go and try to get to my room either when he gets there or before him. If I know him, he'll take his time to scope out who is watching before he does that. He's predictable. Go ask her for an autograph. Then tell her that you're happy to see her and Callum making a go at it since he was recently named one of the country's sexiest bachelors. Just chat her up and mention that she is an understandable woman with Callum's penchant for other women. Make sure you let her know that you saw him leaving with his ex, me. Say that if she doesn't believe you, that you would show her. I'll be riding that stallion when you open our hotel room. I want her to get an eyeful. We good?" Tessa asked.

Both women smiled and gave her the thumbs up.

"You're diabolical," Emmie said.

"Diabolical enough to tank his life with her, sending her back to Vegas and him right back into my arms as he recovers from her dropping him. She doesn't appear to be the type to deal with seeing her man all up in another woman. What is she twenty-eight? She'll find someone else. Callum is mine."

.

# 2

Waking up to someone shaking his shoulder left Callum confused and startled. It took him a minute to remember where he was. His thoughts, while sleeping, had taken him back to that night a year ago when his life had been turned upside down. A year later, he was in the midst of another life-altering scenario. Rubbing his eyes to clear his mind, he sat up straight in the chair in the hospital room and looked up to find Byrum staring down at him. Looking beyond his brother, he stood quickly and almost fell to the floor. He looked over at the two white cribs which were now empty. He didn't see his sons. When he fell asleep, his babies were together in one crib asleep with wires hooked up to various parts of their bodies. How could he have missed any movement of them with him right here in their room. He rubbed his face down the three-day old stubble that had grown in during a time when he refused to leave the hospital for any reason. His heart took a dive as he moved about hysterically trying to remember what should be the scene but wasn't. He shouldn't be alone with just him and Byrum. He should be looking to the faces of two little boys who looked exactly like him. Twins, though not fraternal, they weren't where they were supposed to be. He was about to lose his mind with worry.

"Where are they?" he yelled.

Byrum grabbed him by the arm and steadied him as Callum searched the cribs as if his sons would suddenly reappear in them.

"Callum, they're good. Calm down. You have been asleep for a long time; quite a few hours, according to Kendra. The nurses came to take the boys down for some tests. Kendra and her mother are with them. I need you to calm down before you have a heart attack. Then you'll need your own doctor," Byrum said, in his attempt to lighten the mood in the room.

Callum was furious as he hurried to put his shoes on to go find his sons. Finn and Liam, not here when he woke up was not a good thing. He had tried to get sleep through the days and nights of being at the hospital. Not one time, before this moment, had he been so tired that he didn't hear any commotion in the room. Never had he wanted to be more of a light sleeper than today.

"Why the hell wouldn't someone wake me when they came to get them. Are they okay?" he said, rushing his words out, his body and mind all over the place with worry.

"Cal, stop it. If anything were seriously wrong, do you think that I, or any of us, would not have made sure you were awake? Calm the hell down and let me explain," Byrum demanded, still holding him tight to steady him.

As the oldest brother, usually when Byrum spoke, he and Tellum would listen. Callum was too anxious to do that right now. He needed to go check on his sons. They could be in a position that they needed him and he wasn't there. Any time they woke and looked around, he saw peace come over his sons when their eyes landed on him. He knew that they felt safe.

"Get out of my way, Byrum. They might be scared. I don't have time for this. More than that, this isn't the time for one of your speeches. Where did they go?" he asked, trying to move beyond Byrum yet again.

"If you would just wait a damn minute, I will tell you. Stop,"

Byrum said and put his hands up to let Callum know that he wasn't going to move.

"Okay, talk."

Callum could feel rage entering his body as Byrum talked in circles in the large hospital room. The space with all of its equipment with room for the two twin size beds that were brought in for him and Kendra was closing in on him. All his mind could show him was his boys in distress while he was sleeping.

"It's just tests, Callum; routine tests that could not be done in the room. They took them for body scans to look at their hearts. Both of your sons are fine. There was nothing wrong. After two-months of them being here and after two surgeries each, you know Dr. Clayton Myers said that they are on the mend. They are six-months old and getting bigger and stronger every day. Mom is here. She said when she came in and you were sleeping soundly, she didn't want anyone to wake you unless it was necessary. You and Kendra have been pretty much living here at the hospital. From the looks of you, there hasn't been much by way of showering and changing clothes for you either. I'm thinking that you could also use a shave and a haircut. I promise you, I would not have let you sleep through an emergency when it comes to your sons. This is me. Even if it was Tellum, mom or dad or even Kendra and anyone in her family, why would you think we would do that to you?"

Byrum held up a navy-blue Nike duffle bag.

Callum shook off his anxiety and finally cleared his mind. This was Byrum; one of two brothers who would always be in his corner. He wouldn't take this moment to start being concerned about whether they were looking out for him or not.

"You're right. I'm sorry. It's just that I woke up and didn't see or hear them. I got scared. Since they've been here, especially after the heart surgeries, when I get up to make sure they can see and hear me, they are looking right at me with their big light gray eyes or if they are sleeping, I can see peace on their faces. Just now, I could only see terror when they were nowhere in sight. You have to understand that. I know Tru isn't your son, but you're a father-figure in his life. Remember how crazy you were when he fell off of that jungle gym at the park back in Detroit? Keiko said you were a wild man, running with him in your arms claiming you would run all the way to the hospital if you had to. I heard that story," he said, finally smiling as his heart stopped racing. Callum found himself finally able to relax.

"You're right. I was trying to tell you what was going on as soon as I woke you. I figured you'd been asleep long enough after they were taken down. I didn't want to leave you here asleep with no one around to tell you what was going on."

Callum sat back down after taking the duffle bag and looking through it.

"You're leaving?" he asked Byrum.

"Not right now. I'm headed to *Quiet Whisper* to take another look around. The construction company took me on a tour to show me the amazing progress they are making. I love it all. You've been doing a great job, especially with everything going on."

"That's because you and Tellum fly in to check up on things often. That gives me the time I need to be here at the hospital. Besides, I think that of all of the leadership teams we have at the three resorts, I have the best one. When I check in, there have only been minor issues which are generally handled immediately. In other words, my team is better than yours."

Byrum chuckled and gave him a playful middle finger.

"You wish you had the best team. We all know that my team at *Silent Whisper* is the number one team. You do have quite a team here too, but they are second to mine. You have double the staff that what Tellum and I have at the other resorts. None of us can top our Detroit team. "

"Even though *Quiet Whisper* is one name, I'm actually overseeing two resorts; the adult-only and the family-friendly resort. That makes my resort twice as big as *Secret Whisper* and *Silent Whisper*. I plan to win our bet for the most amazing resort once we have our grand opening here."

"You sure are competitive for a dollar bet. You're right though. You're doing big things here; that's for sure. The progress here is remarkable; I will give you that. I saw Dr. Myers a few minutes ago. I'm glad I could be here for one of his many trips to see after the boys. He's feeling pretty good about their progress."

Callum's regular breathing pattern was back. Byrum was the perfect choice of the person to wake him. He would have run all over anyone else.

"Yeah, he is the best. He's also patched us in to some great doctors out of Johns Hopkins Hospital in Baltimore. That's where he spent most of his years for his residency, I believe, or something like that. If it wasn't for him and his team, I don't know what would have happened to the boys. I'm focused on their care, but still blown away that Kendra kept them from me for a few months. Not only that but how self-involved was I that I didn't know she was pregnant?"

"You know all about them now. That matters. You can't go back in time and change that. I got a chance to see them before they were taken for their tests. They are picking up weight pretty good. I guess feeding isn't a problem."

"They do good with bottle time. The doctor wants us to start introducing them to solid food to fill their bellies now that they are feeling better. The weight loss that signaled a problem has finally shifted. They love milk, but Kendra is getting exhausted trying to feed them both. Her body is going through a lot with breast feeding while also pumping for times when I feed them so that she can rest. She doesn't want the hospital supplementing with formula, so she works overtime to provide for them. She's a remarkable mother."

Callum rubbed his hand down his face again and thought about a shave. He didn't want to rub the rough hair on his chair against his sons. He could definitely use a shave.

"Our cousin, Koko who owns that barbershop will be here to give you a haircut and shave, if you're down for that. I didn't think you would want to go too far from here. Since your condo isn't far, I figured I would take up residence here so that you could go and do that. I'll wait around until you come back."

"Good looking out. I will as soon as the boys are back and I get an update. I can't believe I slept so long. I remember waking up around five in the morning to check on them. Kendra was knocked out over there. Finn was asleep but Liam was wide awake and trying to get out of the crib. Whenever they see me or Kendra, they want out."

"They still have them together in one crib? The other one doesn't look like it's being used."

"Yeah. They do much better together. When the nurses tried to separate them into two separate cribs, they look over at each other and cry like someone was hurting them. When they put them back together, they would immediately stop crying and would tussle with each other and fall asleep touching in some way. It's the cutest thing. They said there wasn't a health issue leaving them together if that helps with them getting healthier. All the wires connected to them are taped down good and covered up. They are curious about them and have often reached for them."

"How is Kendra doing? Or rather, how are you and Kendra doing. It's been a few months since she first arrived?"

"Doing good. Everything has been fast-paced since that first day. They were whisked into the emergency room and examined. Scans were done quickly before we got the bad news. Dr. Myers kept us calm with his optimism. Finn and Liam are not his first patience with the same heart condition I was born with. I told us that they'll be up and moving around soon like nothing is wrong."

"Are you here all night, every night? If so, that's a lot."

"We don't always stay every night here together. We take turns. She's staying at my condo along with her mother and their family when they are here. I'm staying at one of the apartments at *Quiet Whisper* that's been upgraded. We're communicating, but pretty much only about the boys. I've tried to talk to her about what happened, but she doesn't want to. She only wants to focus on why we are here. I'm giving her that."

He didn't admit that they were here because he got her pregnant before she caught him having sex with Tessa. That resulted in Kendra walking out of his life; probably permanently if she hadn't been pregnant with is children and needed him once their heart issues were discovered. No matter the reason, they are here now. This hospital was like a second home for them. They were making it work. Thankfully, the hospital staff was used to having parents who refused to leave as long as their kids were here. They didn't hesitate to bring in two beds for him and Kendra. The hospital even provided some toiletries for them.

"Give her time, Callum. That had to be hard for her seeing you like that with Tessa."

Callum looked toward the door to be sure Kendra wasn't within earshot.

"I know. I will never be able to do enough to get that image out of her head. To know that Tessa set that up was wild."

"Don't blame it all on her. You should not have been anywhere near Tessa that night or any night."

"I know, I know. I'm not that Callum anymore. You know that. That dose of reality that night woke me up faster than you did today. I don't blame Tessa for setting me up. I also don't blame Kendra for walking in on me and Tessa. I'm to blame for thinking with the wrong head, as I always do. That time, I screwed up royally."

"I do know that you've changed," Byrum agreed.

"Kendra doesn't see it. It's been over a year. Every time she sees me, that's all she sees; me with Tessa on top of me. I mean, I didn't even hear the hotel door open. My eyes were closed, because, well – I was enjoying the ride. When I heard a sound and saw Kendra standing there, shocked and disappointed, I couldn't move. Tessa wouldn't stop moving. She even made sure she locked eyes with Kendra. When I tried to get up and go after Kendra when she ran out, Tessa's laugh was haunting. It was all a blur. That's when I drank the rest of the night before you came and grabbed me up. You know how hard I've tried to make amends with her all this time. To know that she went through an entire pregnancy and birth of twins and I didn't know it, crushed me. I even tried to go back through social media to find out anything. All I found were references to her deciding that she wasn't going to play ball anymore. After that, she went into, what looks like hiding. She kept that secret close to her heart. So did her family and her friends. With phone cameras everywhere, I can't believe that no one captured her with a belly. She showed me pictures a few days after she arrived here. She was even more beautiful pregnant. I missed all of that, including their birth. I'm here every day now because I will not miss anything else with them"

"No progress on the two of you finding your way back to at least a friendship for the sake of your sons?"

"We have that. We are working together for their good. Of course, that's a given."

"Ah, I get it. You want more. You want Kendra back."

Callum shook his head up and down and then lowered it.

"I've always wanted her back. That never went away because she cut off all communication with me. When I tried to find her, she had moved. No one in her family would talk to me or give me information on her whereabouts. If I had known she was pregnant, I would have had a private investigator find her. I didn't know. She knew she was pregnant that night in Chicago when she found me with Tessa. She knew I was in Chicago and she wanted to surprise me."

"You were the one surprised, though."

"Yes, I was. I have had regrets every single day since then. I wish I could take that time back but I can't. I can only go forward. Other than when it comes to the boys, she won't let me in. I'm a different man. That night shook me to my core. I know what I messed up. I am hoping she won't make me pay forever."

"If you want her, nothing will stop the two of you from working it out. She's here in Honolulu. You have time to show her more of who you are now. Make sure she understands how sorry you are. I'm pulling for you, brother."

"Is Tellum still here? He came in a few days ago, ahead of you. He took on a lot of work for me while he was here. I know he wanted to get back to Cheyenne and Talia."

His niece was the apple of Tellum's heart.

"He left early this morning. He is how I knew you were finally getting some sleep. We connected before his jet took off. He said to tell you he would check on you in a few days. He also said, keep the daily texts coming on how the boys are coming along. If you need him, he'll be here before your next blink."

Callum smiled and looked up as he stood.

"Because we roll like that," he exclaimed.

"Yes, we do and always will. I saw a news article that talked about Kendra and how sick the twins are. It noted how you're the father, of course, and how you brought in the best cardiothoracic surgeons in this country."

"Yeah, Kendra told me about that. She said she wasn't quoted. Must have been a leak here at the hospital. I will say, Dr. Myers brought in that team that consisted of his wife and his best friend, Sabastian. There were also two doctors from Baltimore. Finn and Liam are getting the best care possible."

"You're woke," Kendra said, walking into the room.

"Where are the boys?" Callum asked walking around Byrum to give her a hug.

"On their way up. You know hospital rules. I can't come up in the same elevator to the pediatric floor. All guests, even parents, have to go through three security checkpoints anytime we want to enter the floor. I love that level of security except for when it comes to watching that elevator door close with them inside and me having to go to another wing to get here."

"How did the tests go?" he asked.

Kendra looked to Byrum and walked over to give him a hug.

"You're still here?" she asked. "I thought you had a meeting or something," she added.

"I did. This fool was sound asleep like one of his sleeping sons. I didn't want him to wake up and no one was here. He went ballistic when I shook him awake and he didn't see them. I knew that would happen. I know my brother."

"Yes, you do. I can only imagine the terror he went through. Sorry, Callum. I should have gotten you up before they were taken out. You get so little sleep these days between being here all the time while also getting work done at the resort."

"Have you seen the resort?" Byrum asked her.

"No, not yet."

"I'm hoping to give her a tour soon," Callum said. "The tests?" he asked her again.

"Oh, right. We won't have all of the results yet, but the doctors are smiling with great optimism. They're coming to give us a better update because I told them you were here in the room. Besides, it's bath time, your favorite time of the day," Kendra said, smiling over at him.

Callum loved every time she smiled in his direction. Those times seldom happened when she first arrived. He was getting more and more of them probably because the boys were improving.

Byrum's laugh filled the room.

"Bath time? This guy? Callum? He hated taking his own baths as a kid. My parents would have to chase him around the house the minute he heard the tub water running. He would kick and scream for the entire bath. Now he's happy giving baths to his sons? I love it!" Byrum joked.

Callum thrust his middle finger up and the group of them laughed.

"I saw that, Callum," their mother said from the doorway.

Byrum laughed and pointed at him as they did when they were kids when one of them got in trouble.

"Sorry about that, mom. I'm glad you're still here. I thought you were going to spend the day with aunt Luna."

"My sister is going to wait until I get there for the day we're planning to catch up. I'll be here one more day before I'm heading back to Detroit. Your father went on a business trip to New York. I want to arrive back home when he does. Let me know if you need me here longer? Kendra's mom and I cleaned up the condo this morning. We also picked up some things for the boys and for you, Kendra. Your mother put them away. I know she's leaving to join your father on the road with his team in a few days. Don't hesitate to let me know if you need me for anything. I love coming to visit with my grandsons. I go from no grandchildren to four, easily," she quipped.

"Four?" Kendra asked.

"Oh, besides Finn and Liam, of course there is Talia, Tellum and Cheyenne's little girl. I also count Keiko's son, Tru, as one of my grandchildren. He loves calling me grandma. He reminds me that after Byrum and Keiko's wedding here at *Quiet Whisper*, I will officially be his grandma. I remind him that I am already that. That makes four. I love all of them equally. Did the tests go well?" Felicia asked.

"Yes. They're on their way back to the room. I'm hoping that I can get news soon that they are healthy enough to travel. I want to get back home to Vegas and start looking into doctors there for them."

No one spoke after that. All eyes turned to Callum who was the most stunned. He had no idea she was planning to take the boys to Las Vegas. What was he going to do now?

# 3

"Mom, you're going to miss your flight!" Kendra yelled as she exited the master bathroom with a towel wrapped around her body. She'd just finished a much-needed shower. It wasn't too often that she was willing to leave the hospital for more than a few hours at a time. Thankfully, she could get away during the day because Callum offered to stay so that she could step away to take care of herself. She also wanted to make time for her mother before she flew out of Hawaii. Having her on an extended stay to be comforting and supportive was necessary. Kendra's mental capacity over her sons' health needed had her in need of her mother's daily hugs, love and confirmations.

Her family has been wonderful by sacrificing their own schedules to fly in and out of Hawaii to check on her and the boys.

She walked into the kitchen to make a cup of coffee and towel-dried her hair. She was enjoying the coconut and vanilla smell that wafted across her nose of the body shower gel that her mother and Callum's mother had brought for her. Finding two cases of it made her day. It was her favorite scent. That along with four large bags of clothes and other toiletries had her wanting for nothing as far as what she needs. What really made her day, as she looked at the sofa in the large family room, were the twenty or so outfits for both boys along with pampers, toiletries, bibs, little shoes, undershirts and other things she would need. She was going to have to figure out a way to get everything back to Vegas when she left in less than a week.

"I'm just about ready," Melissa Grimes said as she walked out of one of the bedrooms rolling two suit cases with her.

"I'm making coffee. Do you want a cup?"

"I do, my dear daughter. You had me up most of the night talking. I'm glad you came back here with me early this morning. You needed that nap, even if it was only two hours. Promise me after I leave that you will get more sleep than you've been getting. Callum is doing a good job looking after them despite his schedule at the resort. He's a great dad, huh?" Melissa asked.

Kendra didn't respond right away. Her mouth and heart wanted to shout that he's a wonderful man, period. He was so different than she ever could have imagined. She knew the single bachelor Callum whom she could not see as a father. She had to admit, she had an idea of him that was all kinds of wrong. He truly did step up to the plate without hesitating. He was on top of things from the moment she landed. From the second she had reached out to him when she found out how sick the boys were, he'd been by her side. She knew that the moment she'd been told how sick the twins were that she had to find Callum. Against the doctors in Las Vegas recommendations, she got them on a private plane to Hawaii after confirming that's where Callum was. She could no longer keep them from him. She knew she had to get their sons to him. He would know what to do. She needed his help in saving them.

Briefly, she forgot about all that had gone on between them. She let go of the image with him and Tessa having sex. Her only focus became her two precious baby boys who needed their father. She needed him too, though she would never admit to that. She kept the focus of what she and Callum were together when it came to the boys. That's how it started and that's how it currently was. When her mother cleared her throat loudly, she knew that she was still waiting for an answer.

"Yes, he's a wonderful father. The boys adore him. Have you seen how they light up for him? They love bath time with him. I love pumping all the extra milk just so that he can feed them and not just me."

"You forgot to note that they are triplets. I swear, did you even have a hand in making them? Were you really there? They look like mini-Callums. Even if he wanted to say that there was a question, he would lose that battle as soon as he opened his mouth. Those boys are all Blackstone, true and through. It's good seeing all of you together."

Kendra knew where that last notion was heading. She stopped that thought immediately. She wouldn't allow her mother to take her there.

"Mom, there is nothing there anymore. Don't go there. You know how I feel. You know what he did to me."

"Yes. I also know that you still love him. You didn't have to have his kids, even after what happened."

"Mom, I would never have chosen any option other than having them. I admit, it crossed my mind. I mean, I was in the midst of going back to a winning basketball team. I thought about not going through with the pregnancy. That lasted all of one second. I gave up my career because I wanted to. I didn't have to. Did I tell you that I have been getting offers to join the coaching staff of two teams? I'm sure my name, by being the daughter of the legendary NBA player, Anthony Sidney Grimes, didn't hurt during their scouting. I wouldn't have to travel a lot with the team to away games. If I did, Amelia wants to help me with the boys."

"Your sister loves them as if they were her own. Still, I don't want her doing that with her time. She needs to finish school. She thinks shifting the virtual college classes will free her up so that she can do more with you and help you more. She needs to stay on campus and focus. I've got you covered with time and anything else you need from me."

"I told her that. Right now, I'm not even thinking about anything work or basketball related. My babies need me. I just want to get home and get settled in. I feel so out of sorts living in the midst of Callum's life these past few months."

Her mother walked into the kitchen and picked up the cup of coffee she'd filled for her. They sat together at the long black marble-topped island with gold specks throughout. The high-back chairs were a perfect match in color with black leather seating, gold accents. The high-backs with the first initial of Callum's last name engraved in the back of the leather was unique and all him.

She was going to miss the condo when she went back home. She had been here before with Callum during their time together. When they wanted to slip away after her team had won the championship, he whisked her off here. They had indulged in a week of loving on every surface in his condo. When she thought back to it, that had been during the time that the boys were conceived. It was the only time they'd been intimate without protection. Callum thought that his pullout game was going to be strong. Her body's grip on him said otherwise. She wasn't concerned since she was on birth control. They had gone together to her doctor to get tested for everything before they made the decision to go without condoms sometimes. Clearly, her birth control pills were not as effective as she thought.

Everywhere she looked, she saw remembrances of them intwined together in one way or another. A few times since arriving in Hawaii, she longed to spend that kind of time with him again. She hadn't been with another man since Callum. Her body still craved his touch, his feel, his loving. She would never speak that out loud. She was too busy still holding him responsible for her broken heart.

"I can't believe you're thinking about leaving here next week," her mother said.

"Why? Last week, the doctors said they could be discharged with strict instructions for their care. As soon as I select a heart doctor and a general primary care pediatrician for them, I can connect all the doctors together. They will share records and outcomes. Being here was never going to be permanent; you know that. At the time when I decided to bring them here, I was scared. I was afraid that I would lose them. I couldn't let that happen and Callum never know about them. Thankfully, nothing happened that made the situation worse. I knew he would know what to do and the right people to connect with."

"Yes, I know that. I didn't expect you to be ready to leave so soon. What is Callum saying?"

"So far, nothing at all. I saw the look on his face when I said I was preparing to go back to Las Vegas now that the boys are stronger. It's time. He needs to get back to his life and so do I. He knows there is an open door for him to always see the boys any time. I would never keep them from him."

"He may be worried about that. You did go through an entire pregnancy and birth and didn't tell him until you needed his help."

Kendra sat her coffee cup on the table and secured the towel around her hair.

"That's not fair."

"Okay, I'm sorry. I'm not trying to say you used him. He is their father. No one would doubt your rationale. I know what he did. Taking them away from him now wouldn't be right, and you know it. You're an adult. You make your own decisions. I know he will take care of them in every way possible. Isn't he paying all the costs?"

"He is. We're not concerned about finances in taking care of them. He's already making provisions for everything they could possibly need now and in the future. I knew he would even if it's not needed. I've got money. I don't have his money, but I don't want for anything. Callum has added them to the insurance his company provides which is the best I've ever seen. They cover everything. I can also select doctors out of network if I want to. He wants all bills sent to him. He doesn't have to do that."

"Kendra, he does. He is their father. Don't try and stick out your chest too far when he's willing to do what a father should do. Do not be so hurt that you look at his support as a crutch. We know that's what this is. Look at the family he comes from. They are amazing, good-hearted people. I can't speak to how Callum is as a mate, but when it comes to his sons, let him do what he wants and not just what you need. He's a parent too. Don't be so strong that you don't see the value in having a loving father for them even if you're not together."

"I'm not doing that, momma. Look, maybe I didn't do things right in the beginning. I was just so hurt. It's still hard to forget and let go of that image. I was in love with him. I didn't expect that."

"I know and I feel for you. I want you to think of what you're doing by separating them from him at this point in their lives. You're not playing ball right now. Financially, you're set. You have the money from your six-year career. You also have your trust fund from your father's career. None of my children have to work. I'm glad all of you want to. TJ is graduating from Harvard next year. Amelia has two more years at Hampton University. You have your degree, after graduating early, from

North Carolina A&T and then going into the WNBA as the number two draft pick. You can do anything you want to do, including doing nothing but being a mother to my grandsons. You can do that from anywhere, unless you have some job back in Vegas that I don't know about. Do you plan on playing ball again?"

"Not anytime soon. I'd like to think about it. I have some other job offers, including anchoring the news with my degree in Journalism I'm also thinking about going back to school online to get my master's degree."

"Baby, the world is your oyster. All that you just said about school, you can do from here. Of course, I'm in Vegas to help you if you find that you just can't be here anymore. You have the support of your father, brother and sister, when they are in town. What I think doesn't matter, I know."

"Mom, do not limit your impact on my life with your suggestions. I hear them all."

"Then hear this; think about your next step before you make a decision. Just think about it. Wherever you are, I will be. You see those boys with their father. If that doesn't tug at your heart, who are you? You are my child and I love you. Think about that image of him with them before you make a choice. If you still want to leave here, I will support you."

Before they could continue, there was a buzz from the front desk on the wall monitor next to the door. Kendra looked at the clock on the wall above the front door.

"That must be the front desk letting us know that your rideshare is here to take you to the airport."

Kendra got up and spoke into the intercom while her mother grabbed for her luggage.

Before she could speak, the doorbell also rang.

"That can't be the driver. They wouldn't be able to get up

here that easily."

Kendra looked into the camera on the wall that showed outside the door. She smiled when she saw Callum's face and his hand waving at the camera.

"It's Callum, mom."

Kendra unlocked and flung the door open.

"Hey!" he said.

"Who is with the boys?" she enthusiastically asked with a hint of fear in her voice.

"They're fine. Leilani is with them. Remember, she's a critical care head nurse. They were sleeping when I left. The condo is five minutes from the hospital if I need to get back there in a hurry. I was hoping to talk to you. Hi, Ms. Melissa. I see you're ready to leave. Oh, your ride is downstairs in front of the building. I think they buzzed up here."

"Oh, thanks Callum. Kendra, I will call you when I get home. Take care of my babies until I see you all again in about a week. Your father has a game in Los Angeles against my favorite team, after his team, that is. I'm going home and then I'll meet him there. Call me if you need anything."

Kendra kissed her mother's cheek and waited while Callum hugged her before she rushed out to the elevator. Now alone, she closed the door behind Callum after he came all the way inside.

"You rang the bell?" she asked. "It's your home. You have a key and the code," she said.

"True, but I don't want to invade your privacy. I'm glad you had these hours today to yourself. You needed that," he said.

Callum walked over and sat on one of the three single brown and gold trimmed chairs in the family room across from the large beige sectional with brown and gold accents. She started to sit on the sectional which was backed up in front of a wall of windows that overlooked the view of the ocean from the thirtieth-floor penthouse condo. There were curtains that could be opened and closed with a remote, but she loved the view. The curtains were always opened.

Callum mentioned to her when he offered to let her stay here that he also loved having the curtains opened all the time. He shared that he felt a sense of peace every time he opened the door and looked out.

She looked at herself and remembered that she was dressed in only a towel. How did she remember? It was the way that Callum was looking at her. She saw his sexy light gray eyes turn to a sensually, erotic-infused darker gray. She knew that look. He was imagining her without her towel. She knew what that felt like. Every time she saw his perfectly toned, muscled body, even with clothes on it, all she thought about was his powerful strokes into her body. They were the kind that drove her from one orgasm to yet another. She wasn't as experienced in that arena as he was, considering before him, she'd only been with one guy while in college. She still liked what she loved. What she loved was the way he never failed to make her body feel incredibly satisfied. She never left his presence, when they were in bed, without her body completely satiated. Even now, she felt a tremble in her legs that had her rushing off to put some clothes on. Her desire to drop her towel in front of him was strong. Hurrying, she slipped a pair of workout yoga pants over her curvy hips and grabbed a sports bra and t-shirt. She then raced back out to where Callum had not moved.

He was sitting comfortably with one leg over the knee of the other. His hands were locked together over his raised knee.

"You're back. You ran out of here like you stole something," he joked.

She smiled and laughed when he attempted to lighten the

mood. He had a knack for doing that when he sensed she was uncomfortable.

"Sorry. I took a shower right before you came. I was trying to make sure you my mom didn't miss her flight. We got caught up in conversation and I forgot I hadn't gotten dressed."

"Either way, you're beautiful, especially in a towel."

"Callum?"

"I know. We agreed to no suggestive language. I can't help it. You're so damn beautiful. Take the compliment," he offered.

"You're right. I'm sorry. Thank you. I'm just a little stressed over the boys."

The conversation stopped when there was a soft knock on the door. They looked to each other questionably.

"Your mom?" he asked.

"I don't know."

Kendra moved toward the door, but Callum beat her to it. He looked in the camera and it wasn't her mother he saw. He opened the door.

"Hey, Callum? Where have you been? I haven't seen you in a minute?" the beautiful, elegant woman who stood on the other side of the door said.

Kendra's jealous meter shot up to the stars. She was gorgeous; just Callum's type. She wondered how long it would be before one of his women barged in here. She turned and went into the kitchen to avoid their interaction.

"I will call you. I haven't forgotten. We have to do this another time, okay?" he asked her.

"Uh, yeah, sure."

Callum closed the door. Kendra didn't look his way. She, instead, spoke to him over her shoulder.

"Same old Callum, I guess. How many of your women will show up here? I really need to get back to Vegas," she said, speaking harshly.

"Turn around, Kendra. I am not going to speak to your back. We are not kids."

She turned sharply and placed the coffee mug hard down on the counter.

"I guess she didn't know I would be here? I'm usually at the hospital this time of day."

"Her presence is not what you think."

"Oh? There has been a lot of things not being what I think when it comes to you. This was just another."

"Can you just listen without jumping to conclusions? That was Jocelyn. She's a member of my staff. She is also very happily married to a Hawaiian man who would have any man for dinner who looked at his wife suggestively. She also has three kids, all under the age of five. She asked me about being able to switch to the team that works on the family-friendly resort so that she could be closer to her daughter, the youngest of the group, who attends the daycare there. It would be easier for her to get to her for visits during the day. I was working on that around the time that you arrived here with the boys. I forgot about that request. I need to make a note to have someone on my team make that change immediately. She's not one of my, what you call, women. There are no women. I haven't had time for anything but you and the boys."

Kendra dropped her hunched up shoulders and looked away from his sexy gaze. There was no way for him to look at anyone other than in that way. He was so freaking gorgeous.

"I'm sorry. I didn't know."

"You're right. You didn't and that's okay. Can we talk about why I'm here?"

"Okay," she said softly. "I'm really sorry, Callum."

"I get it. I know why."

"What did you want to talk about?"

"You leaving here and going back to Vegas. I know that's your plan. I haven't said anything before now. Time is winding down. Today, I was told that they are getting released, maybe tomorrow. I'm hoping I can convince you to reconsider leaving with them. I know we aren't together. We have spent all of our time making sure they were okay. Now that they are, I'm sure, like me, you're wondering what's next."

"I am," she uttered quietly.

"Stay. Please think about staying here. The boys aren't out of the clear completely. They are just well enough to come home with us. You know I have to be here for the resort development. I want to be able to help you with them; anything you need for and with them, I want to be a part of. You came here to me when you needed me. Now, I need you. I need you and them to be close. I don't want to sound selfish. I know in your mind, I don't deserve asking for anything from you. I love them more than life. I haven't had time to think about what my world would now look like if they were in Vegas with you. I have loved having them here; I am loving having you here. Their doctors are here, though I know you can get new ones. We can get any doctors we want for them. I can get additional help around here with them. Leilani has offered to come through during the week to check their vitals and to see how they're doing in between appointments. I'm planning to add more security now that social media knows we're all here. Everyone wants the story. I feel like we're A$AP Rocky and Rihanna, there is so much attention on us. Here, you will get the privacy I know you want. The boys will be safe from flashing lights and people in our business. You can stay here and I will continue to live on the grounds of the resort. I can be here as much as I am now; even more. I don't want to be away from them. Please, reconsider."

This is what Kendra feared. She dreaded having this moment of looking in to his eyes as he pleaded with her to not go back to Vegas. She was all set until her mother spoke in one ear and now Callum is in the other. Could she really take them away from their father now that they woke up looking for him every day? Could she go back to Vegas with this desire building up in her to be near him again as more than him being the father of her children? On the other hand, could she be so cruel as to still be angry enough at him to not consider his feelings? Her mother was right. That person she was thinking of is not who two loving parents raised. She and her siblings had the best life growing up around both of their parents just as she knew Callum and his brothers did. She didn't have to go back to Vegas. It was a want; a desire.

What she knew she was fighting was her growing attraction to Callum again. Seeing him in father mode being so loving and caring reminded her of why she had fallen in love with him years ago, though she never told him. She didn't have a chance to. She'd caught him inside of another woman. Her love for him had shattered into a million pieces. Disappointing her mind but feeding her heart, she was still in love with him. She couldn't leave.

"I'll stay," she said.

"You will?" Callum asked her eagerly, rushing over and picking her up off of her feet.

"Yes!" she shouted and laughed as he turned around in circles with her in his arms.

That moment of them enjoying a happy moment was short-lived when he placed her back down on her feet, bringing them body-to-body and face-to-face.

She didn't look away when Callum's eyes dropped from hers down to her lips. She could feel her breaths quicken at what his look meant. She knew. It was in her as well. Would he kiss her?

Callum's breathing increased as his mouth moved closer to hers. She figured he was going slow in order to see if she would move away, giving her an out. She didn't want one. She didn't take one. She stood her ground and allowed her own eyes to take full stock of his lips. She was suddenly remembering what those lips could do to hers; and not just her lips.

Those lips had once loved and caressed every part of her. The sexy sensation vibrating up from between her legs was a sign that her body remembered all of him. She waited through the quiet, yet salaciously intensified moment. When Callum finally kissed her lips, she didn't move. She didn't join him. Then he kissed her lips sweetly again. When he came to her for a third kiss, she returned the kiss with a fervent one of her own.

She avidly went after his lips in the same hungry manner that he went after hers. They were caught up. Nothing else mattered but the feel of his lips on hers. The lip lock was spicy. It held all the promises it used to hold as a prelude to the best loving of her life. She gave as good as she got, desiring him; wanting him. The passion that had once fused them was back in this kiss. He tasted good. He felt good against her. Her heart battered against the insider of her chest. Would she ever not want him with everything in her? She wondered if the passion would always be this hot. Do people walk around in a state of longing as she seems to always do?

Callum pulled away, but kept his hands on the side of her face where he had moved them when their tongues found each other. All the sexy feels didn't let them forget how good they were when they shared a zealous kiss like the one they'd just had. Kissing always took their need to the next level. All it took was the feel of their lips.

"I won't apologize for that," he said. "I know how you feel

about me. I have been dying to kiss you since the moment you got off that plane that first day. I'm sorry for what I did. I know that won't make up for anything. I just want to keep saying I'm sorry. I also want to thank you for staying here with the boys. How about we head back to see them and then we can grab a bite to eat during their next nap. Let's talk about what you staying here looks like. You can redecorate this place any way you want. Turn one of the bedrooms into their room. Buy whatever you want. Do whatever you want. I want you to feel at home here. We can let their doctors know that you're staying here with them so that we can start getting on the schedule for appointments with their doctors. Thanks for staying. Also, thanks for not slapping me when I kissed you. You stay tasting delicious, huh? Shall we head out?"

Kendra couldn't find any words. When he walked away and went back to sit in the family room, she nodded her head and went to get her phone and her purse. In the bedroom, she went in search of her shoes. She needed this space between them as she let her mind attempt to navigate if more kisses were in store for them. If so, what did they mean? What could it lead to? Was she ready and open to find out? Her heart was saying yes. Her body was yelling yes. Her mind was being cautious. She was in it now. She had agreed to stay. Whatever came next, she had to be ready for.

# 4

These days, Callum enjoyed his casual strolls through the halls of the hospital, the place that was as much home for him as his apartment. Though they were a week behind when he and Kendra thought they would be able to bring Finn and Liam home, he wouldn't and couldn't complain about them still being here getting care from a great medical team. He waved and whispered hellos to everyone who had come to know him and Kendra as if they were all a part of a family. He got and gave air high-fives from some people, thumbs up from others and actual hugs from a few as he headed in the direction of the pediatric ward. He was anxious to hear what Kendra had called him to the hospital for. He was planning to come through anyway. Once she reached out, he made everything else secondary. He was still dressed in a dark gray suit, light green shirt and a matching tie still tight around his neck. He had spent the whole morning in meetings and walking through the resort. He had an extra pep in his step today because both of his brothers were in Hawaii.

Tellum flew in early in the morning for all of the meetings, especially the one with their accounting firm. They wanted to hear first-hand about all the numbers that were being run with the large expenses they incurred with the additional land that was purchased. That property had recently been excavated. They were moving ahead. Construction on the additional bungalows, small cottages and hotel rooms had already begun.

They could see the beginnings of some incredible dwellings that were sure to draw visitors from right here on Hawaii to countries far away. They looked forward to welcoming them all.

After the meetings, Tellum had made a quick stop at the hospital to check on the boys with his own eyes before rushing to the airport. He was taking a few weeks off to spend quality time with Cheyenne and his baby girl, Talia. He had certainly earned that. If they weren't too careful, they could all get caught up in their desire to have and build more and better. What had to come first, was family. Being a father, Callum was making his own changes to make his kids and Kendra a priority.

Byrum and Keiko were both here as well. With the construction noises happening, they opted to stay at a hotel instead of at the resort. Their plan was to stay for one more day after he took them on a tour of the event hall where their wedding and reception would take place. Keiko wanted another look now that she was getting closer to making final plans with her event planner for all of the decorative ideas she has for the space. He was looking forward to kicking back with them at dinner at a local restaurant later that night. First, he did what was a priority for him; he was heading to see his family.

Callum smiled, knowing that when he thought of his family, he wasn't just speaking of the boys. That sentiment also included Kendra. They hadn't shared much other than a few curious, yet sexy glances since that kiss a week ago. He wanted to venture into more, but with the little setback with the boys not coming home as expected, they were refocused on making sure they were on track to great health. He, himself, had been on this same medical path as a baby. He survived and so would his sons.

The doctors reassured them that they were simply being cautious. Since Kendra decided to stay on the island, the hospital didn't worry about making sure they got them ready to travel to Las Vegas with a medical team onboard just in case. With the heart problems, putting the twins on a plane had to be monitored. Since they were staying in Hawaii, everyone wanted to get another look at them. They also wanted to plan out additional appointments and therapy going forward. Callum was okay with that as long as they weren't taking precautions out of fear of something going wrong that as their parents, he and Kendra were not made aware of. He wanted to know everything.

Though he wanted to breach the subject with Kendra of rekindling what they had started in the past, he let that go in order to stay tuned into what was happening to their sons first. Any need, desire or thirst he had for her, which he knew would never die, would have to be put on the back burner for now. He could wait. She has been, was and always would be. After all, he'd waited all this time. He only wanted her and no one else. Time was on his side since she made the decision to say in Hawaii. He had to figure out how to convince her that flexing as if he could do anything he wanted and still have her was his first mistake.

Callum went through the three checkpoints that were required before being allowed on the final elevator that took him to the right floor. Once inside, he leaned is head back against the elevator wall and closed his eyes. He was beyond tired. His days were spent going between work and the hospital. His nights were spent, most evenings at hospital, with some spent at the apartment when he and Kendra decided to split the schedule of spending the entire night at the hospital. Since she had more free time than he did, she took most of the shifts, especially at night. He loved coming by to give the boys their baths before their evening dinner. He loved rocking them to sleep.

Thankfully, they both did good sleeping through the night. Even when the nurses had to come in to disturb their sleep to get vitals or just to check on them, both boys easily settled back down and went back to sleep. Their routine was working.

Getting off of the elevator, he was greeted by a nurse who halted saying hello. Callum could not hold in a big yawn if he was paid to do so. She waited through that before greeting him. Everyone knew who he was and that he was behind the resort development. No one questioned how tired he was all the time.

"I do believe every time I see you, you are in the middle of the world's biggest yawn. You need to get more sleep," she said.

"I know and thank you. I'm working on it. It's hard to do these days."

"I get that. I drive past the construction every day when I come to work and go home. I told my husband that I don't care what we needed to sacrifice, when the resort opens, I want to get a room for a few nights. It's beyond time for us to enjoy a place to hang out that doesn't allow kids. I love all of my children; I swear I do. I just need a break every now and then," she said.

"I get it. That's why my brothers and I are building this place. We also offer a huge discount for Hawaiian residents. Make sure you ask about that whenever you book."

"Thanks Mr. Blackstone. Your resort is all the talk around all of the islands. People are always talking about how they are already saving for a staycation. It's exciting. We've all seen the stories about the other two resorts, *Secret Whisper* and *Silent Whisper*. They are the places to be. I know some people in Hawaii don't like all the visitors, but I love it. The good thing is between your resorts and all the jobs you're created and the foundation your family has set up to benefit Hawaiian's, all I see is goodness coming from the development. The construction can be a lot, but you have to have that to get to the greatness that it will be."

"That's good to know and a great way to look at things. Hi, everyone!" Callum greeted as he walked past the first of two nurse's stations.

"Hi, Mr. Blackstone," they all chanted and waved as he walked by. At the end of the hall, right outside of the boys' room, stood Kendra. She was the perfect sight for him after a long workday. He had hoped to get by sooner. She looked happy to see him despite how late he was. He walked right up to her.

"I'm sorry I'm so late," he explained to her.

When he got close, she surprised him by taking both of his hands in hers, cocking her head to the side and smiling up at him.

"It's okay. I understand your work. I was here with them. They are waiting for you. I think every time someone walks in their room and they look to the door, they are hoping it's you."

"Well, this time it will be. How are they? You said you had great news for me?" he asked.

"Yes. They can come home tomorrow. Can you believe it?" she cheered.

Callum lit up as bright as the busiest Christmas tree.

"What happened? They did the four hours?"

He remembers that Dr. Myers said that he decided he wanted the boys to have four hours on and four hours off of the heart monitors. He wanted them free to move about, keeping them busy before hooking the monitors back up to see how they did.

"They did. Even though neither of them is walking yet, though they keep trying, I got them up on their feet and let them walk around until they fussed for me to let them sit down. Their little fat legs were moving. Your sons need to be on a diet," Kendra joked.

"Not on your life. Considering how small they were when they arrived, I love them chunky. So, the test worked well?"

"Oh, the test worked great. They will still need to be monitored while at home for a while, just because they are here and close enough to the hospital that they can monitor them from here. They would have released them today but it's late in the evening. One more night is fine. I'm too happy that they are coming home to be concerned about one more night. What do you think?" she asked.

Callum didn't think. He could only think about doing and so he did. He reached for her chin and held it up, pulling her closer to him. He kissed her with power, lust and as much zeal as he could muster up even though he was dead tired. With the loud construction happening late into the evening, he hasn't been able to get a lot of sound sleep staying on the resort. He got it in where he could. When he released her lips after kissing them lightly first once, twice and then a third time, he hummed against them.

"That's what I think. First of all, you just gave me the best news of my day. Second, thanks for again letting me kiss you. What time tomorrow are they releasing them? I need to check that everything is set at the condo."

"It's all good. When your cousin Leilani came earlier today to sit with me and the boys for a while, she told me to step out for a bit and get some air. I took that time to stop at the condo to wash some clothes and to put down the new rugs for their room that finally came. I think we're good. Your mother sent ten cases of pampers and an equal number of boxes of wipes. She ordered them locally and had them delivered. When I got to the condo, the order had arrived. The main desk staff had everything brought up. I emptied some of the boxes and put the pampers and wipes on the shelves under the changing tables.

There was some other stuff too; some for me and some for you. My mother sent a bunch of stuff too. Our boys will never need for anything with such wonderful grandmothers. Of course, I can't forget about all that you have and are doing for them and for me. I don't know how to thank you."

Callum felt the corner of his mouth turn up into a sexy, sinister grin. He knew what he was thinking. He was sure she wasn't. He leaned close to her ear.

"I'll think of something and get back to you," he said and winked before heading into the room.

"I'm sure you will. I can think of something too," she said under her breath.

Callum turned back in her direction.

"Say something?" he asked.

"Nope. All good," she replied and followed him in.

The second Finn and Liam saw him from behind the gates of their crib, they scramble to try and pull themselves up but couldn't quite get it because they were too excited to focus on standing. All they wanted was their daddy.

"Hey, my boys! You are looking good. Daddy missed you all day long. Uh, I think you're getting taller on me."

Callum leaned over and kissed both of them. That only made them claw for him harder and scream louder when he didn't pick them up right away.

"You know what they want," Kendra said as she walked over and tried to soothe each boy by rubbing their heads full of hair. They wanted no parts. They only wanted their daddy.

"Okay, I'm coming. Daddy has to wash his hands," Callum said, moving fast to get his suit jacket off and roll up his sleeves. He washed his hands thoroughly and quickly. As soon as he dried them, he headed back to their cribs where they were sitting down and really crying now. Every glimpse of him that didn't include them being in his arms always turned to tears.

The nurse tried to help quiet them to no avail.

"I guess only your touch will work," she said.

"That is the truth," Kendra said, agreeing.

Callum reached down with both arms and came back up with two happy and smiling babies in his arms. Both stopped crying and laid their heads on either side of his chest.

"My boys missed me," he said, kissing their heads before sitting in the rocking chair that Tellum and Cheyenne had sent to the hospital. They had to get special permission to have it sent and placed in their rooms. As a thank you to the hospital, they also donated enough of the same chairs to have one placed in every room in the pediatric wing. Cheyenne said that the same chair was a life saver in calming Talia down when she cried. The way his sons calmed, she had assessed the need perfectly.

"Look at them. Yes, they did. They love their daddy a lot! They really light up when you are in the room. Did Ms. Grimes give you the good news?" the nurse asked.

"She did. Are any of their doctors still around? I'd like to speak to one directly if they have the time."

"I believe so. Let me check and I'll send one in. I'm happy they are going home. I will miss their little cute faces and the way they try to hold a conversation. It's cute. Today, they were doing sign language asking for milk. I didn't know what that was until Ms. Grimes told me."

"More signs? I love it. TJ has been here again?" he asked.

Kendra's brother didn't get to see them as much as he wanted but still, he took the time to teach them some American Sign Language.

"He was here on that day last week when you went out of town for business. He wanted to come and keep me company while you were gone. He taught the boys some key signs for their age. Things like, bottle, milk, shoe, uncle and bed. Now they do milk all the time or bottle because they know that brings milk. All day, they've been doing those signs. Oh, TJ also video chatted with them earlier. They just laughed at the screen and kept reaching for it. Having a brother who is partially deaf has taught me that it's important for the boys to learn sign language too. TJ can't wait to become their teacher," Kendra said.

"Well, he'll have to teach me too. Especially when they get older and try to curse me out in sign language. I need to know," Callum joked.

"How was today? Did you get a lot done?"

"Whoa," Callum said as Finn tried to crawl up his body.

"You know what he wants. He loves his head way up on your shoulder. He's been waiting all day for that, I'm sure."

Kendra was about to attempt to help him.

"I got him. I think he's got it. I like that he's learning to use his legs more."

"That's why the tests on and off the monitors has gone so well. They are strong and ready to assert some independence away from being in the crib all the time. That will be good when we get them home. Those new rugs are big, bright and colorful. They have infant activities like a spinning wheel and a mirror that they will love."

"I like the sound of that. I bet they'll love the mini ball pit in the family room. Are you ready to go home with your mommy and daddy?" Callum asked them.

"I know I'm ready. Speaking of tomorrow, what's your work schedule like?"

Callum looked up at her and tried to read what her eyes were saying. Usually, he could read her. Today, she was a blank slate.

"No work tomorrow if they are coming home. In fact, I'll

probably take a few days off. I'll connect with my team at the resort tonight when I get back there. I'll give them an update on my meetings today. They'll know what to do to step in during my absence. They also know how to reach me, Tellum or Byrum, though Byrum will be in the air tomorrow with Keiko going back home to Detroit. I think they are planning to go to *Silent Whisper* for a few days while Tru is with his father. I want to be here when they are released so that I can spend time with them getting settled in at the condo. Is something up?" he asked.

"No. I was going to ask about that. I was hoping you would free up some time."

"Sweetheart, I can free up all of my time for as long as you want me to. If I get too busy with work, just pull me back from that ledge. I think you'll find though, that I plan to do a lot less work and much more time with the three of you. You good with that? I meant to ask if you have signed up for your classes yet? I can work around that time that you need to study so that I have the boys and you can have peace to focus on classes."

"I have. Class starts next week. I'm only taking two classes for now to see how that goes when it comes to two rambunctious little boys being my priority. I should be fine. The nanny will be there early in the day to help me with them. Your cousin is also planning on coming by a lot. Leilani has been a great help. So has the rest of your family here on the island when your parents or my family isn't here. We have so much help."

"That's good."

Callum slowly rocked and before long, both boys were sound asleep.

"Want to put them down?" she asked.

Callum nodded. When Kendra tried to take Finn, his little grip on Callum's shirt and his unhappy grunt meant that he knew what they were trying to do. He wasn't having any of it.

They let them be.

"They're fine. I love holding them."

There was quiet between them. Kendra took the time to straighten up their crib.

"They have two hours before the monitors go back on. I want to do their bath while they don't have them on. I'm going to see if the nurse can bring everything in. I know she went to get two clean wash bins earlier and forgot."

When Kendra turned toward the door, Callum stopped her. He'd been holding in an ask since he arrived. It was now or never.

"Listen, remember I told you that Byrum and Keiko were here?"

"Yes."

"I'm meeting them for dinner in a few hours. I was wondering, if I can get my cousin to come and sit with the boys, would you be interested in going with me?"

She hesitated. He knew he shouldn't have. She wasn't ready.

"What? As your date?"

"Is that so bad?" he asked quickly.

She hesitated again. He wouldn't take back his offer. She would have to tell him no.

"I'd like that. Leilani has a half of a shift here at the hospital. She noted that for me when she stopped by earlier. Do you want me to call and ask her if she can hang around for a bit later?"

"No, I'll do it. I just wanted to be sure you were okay with it before I did so."

"I am. Thanks for asking."

"Thanks for saying yes."

Callum watched her leave out as he settled the boys more comfortably on him. He held them tight, more thankful than ever for them and for Kendra. What was to be for them, he had to work on. He wanted her back. His thirst for her was on a level so high that he couldn't see it with the naked eye. Speaking of naked, his body recognized her. He could see her need for him in her eyes. It's why she made sure to look away when their steamy glances became too much for her. He wouldn't press to satisfy his thirst for her. When she was ready for more with him, he would be right there. He was just happy that the boys would be coming home in a day. They continue to be his best gift ever.

Callum internally kicked himself. He missed so much time with the three of them because he as immature in his personal life as he was mature in the business world. He had to do better if he was going to have what Tellum and Byrum have. There was no comparison needed. It was the happiness in them that he wanted for himself. He was ready to build a personal life that was as big as his business. Doing it alone wasn't an option that sat well with him.

# 5

Byrum and Callum walked ahead of Keiko and Kendra as they exited the restaurant. Kendra felt relaxed after they spent the last three hours laughing, talking and eating some of the best food she'd ever had. The two times she'd ever been to Hawaii had been with Callum. Both times he'd taken her to different places to eat and experience real Hawaiian dishes. This place surpassed her expectations. Besides that, this night was the most relaxed she'd been in a long time.

She'd been around Byrum many times before, but this was her first time getting the chance to converse with Keiko. They really dived in when the talk turned to them being mothers. Keiko gave her a lot of good tips or as much as she could. Even though Keiko only had one child and she had two, the bottom line of her advice was to give herself some grace. She also told her to let others help as much as they would like. She will find that getting in sleep when she needs it will only happen when others step in to assist with the boys. She was definitely going to take that to heart.

"Did you ladies have a good night?" Callum asked as they all waited at the curb for the stretch Mercedes limousine that Callum had secured for the night. That way, no one had to drive. All they had to do was enjoy the ride.

"I did. I can't wait to get married here. Hawaii is beautiful. My event planner showed me how she's going to bring my vision to life. I'm ready to be this man's wife for a lifetime. I've already told him he is it for me. After all we've gone through to be together, including my fear of sleeping with the boss, we will make this love last forever."

"Kendra?" Callum asked.

Her eyes landed on him. Before she spoke, her mind simply said, *fine*. Callum was beyond handsome. He was tall, cocky and confident, beautiful white teeth with the perfect smile and eyes that could reach down into your heart. The word irresistible came to mind. She was so focused on him that she almost missed answering his question.

"Yes, I had a wonderful time. Thanks for inviting me."

"Did I mention how beautiful you are tonight? You are killing it in that purple dress. I love it. Purple is my favorite color," Callum noted.

"Yes. I remember that," she said.

She didn't tell him that after he invited her out, she left the hospital and went straight to a boutique on a recommendation from one of the nurses. It was clear that the choice of the dress was a good one. She captured Callum, most of the night, taking all of her in.

"This night out was a good idea. Kendra and I have been running on empty trying to make sure we were at the hospital anytime we had a break."

"Both of you needed this time. Finn and Liam are doing good. Leilani is keeping a close eye on them, especially when either or both of you need to step away," Byrum said.

"We couldn't do this without all the family," Kendra acknowledged.

Their car pulled up and all four got in.

"Are the two of you heading to the hospital?" Byrum asked once they were seated.

"Only for a few moments. For the first time, we are both staying at our own places tonight. They come home tomorrow. Kendra and I will need some rest tonight. We've got all of these instructions for taking care of them."

"So, you're staying where?" Byrum asked.

"At an apartment on the resort. Kendra is in my condo, which is also where the boys will be. She's got their room all ready for them, including two cribs when I know she's only going to use one," Callum kidded.

"Hey, blame that on your sons. At the hospital, when the nurses try putting them in two different cribs, they cry for each other. When they are together, they also sleep better. It seems their hearts rest better without all the fussing. I have two, just in case, but until they are ready to be separated, one it is," Kendra laughed.

"Has my mother flooded your place with a bunch of baby stuff?" Byrum asked.

"Mom is out of control. I swear she sends these huge boxes of baby stuff every few days. They will never want for anything," Callum explained.

"Between your mother and mine, the boys are set for life; and so am I. I don't have to buy anything. They are well loved," Kendra said.

"So are you," Callum added, his eyes planted squarely on her.

"That I am. When are the two of you leaving?" Kendra asked.

"We were going to leave tonight, but I'm tired. I just want to relax," Keiko said.

"Me too. We've been running around since we arrived. Some quiet time tonight is definitely on the menu," Byrum explained.

The car pulled up to the entrance of the hotel where Byrum and Keiko were staying.

"This is us. Kendra, it's been nice getting to know you. I can't wait to spend more time with the twins. I hope to get back here soon. If not, I hope you'll be at the wedding. I've added your name to the invite list."

Kendra gazed over at Callum to see if he was as surprised as she was to hear Keiko say she was invited to the wedding. He showed no emotion.

"Oh, yes, thank you for that. I would love to come. You are going to be a beautiful bride."

"I know I can't wait to see her that day," Byrum exclaimed. "Callum, I'll call you in the morning before we leave. I want to be sure the boys are on their way home before we take off. Or, call me if they get discharged before I call you. Take care of them. Remember, no work for you for at least a week. I was hoping for more, but I don't feel like the fight. Tellum and I have things covered. You have a great and extremely large team here; use them and us as much as you need to," Byrum added.

"I hear you. I plan to take one, possibly two weeks to just enjoy my family. Thanks for dinner," Callum said.

Kendra hugged Byrum and Keiko as they exited the limousine.

"Where to sir? The hospital?" the driver asked Callum, who moved to the seat next to Kendra where Keiko had been sitting. He turned to her with a question on his face. He was letting her make the decision.

"For a few minutes? I know we're not spending the night with them. I want to get hugs and kisses and then I'll be ready. I feel weird not staying with them tonight."

"If you want to stay with them, then do that. I don't want you tossing and turning about it all night. If you want me to stay with them to help you feel better about it, I will. What do you want to do?"

"A few minutes and then I'm good. I still want to make sure everything is ready for tomorrow. When I'm at the hospital, I'm up and down all night long. I hate to do this but can you stay with them? I know you're probably tired with work and all. I would feel better if you would."

"Of course, I can. That's a given. Let's go up and then I'll see you home before I run home to change into something comfortable. I'll let the nurses know that I'll be back."

"Thanks, Callum. I'll be up first thing in the morning. They said discharge will be around eleven."

"Get some extra rest. There is no telling what our lives will be like when they come home. I want you to be well rested."

"Perfect. You're a great dad, Callum. I know you don't need the pat on the back, but I want you to know that I have no worries because I know the boys have you."

Callum took her hand in his and held on to it.

"You have me too. I know things are odd, but you have me also. The three of you are my life; my everything. This isn't just about them."

Kendra nodded. She couldn't speak. If she did, old feelings would control the conversation. There was a time when a night like tonight would end with them in each other's arms sharing heated kisses and much more. She missed that. She missed him.

She relaxed and let her memories form a smile on her face. Throughout the evening, when her eyes landed on Callum's lips, she thought back to how spontaneous they had been. He would kiss her anyplace, doing it unashamed even in front of strangers. Those lips do something to her every time; even in her memories like now. She looked forward to dreaming tonight. For sure, the night will be filled with thoughts of Callum; just like every other night lately.

**

Callum stood at the door of the limousine watching Kendra slow walk to the car. He felt like she was second-guessing her decision to go home for the night. They spent the last hour with their sons before they were finally down for the night. Knowing that they would be closely monitored, he thought that Kendra felt comfortable enough to leave knowing they would be fine. He was wondering if he should tell her to go back. He would still be back later.

"If you don't want to leave, then don't," he said when she reached him.

She smiled up at him and squared her shoulders in her attempt to let him know she was okay.

"I'm good. I mean, I'm not really sleepy right now, but I'm sure once I am, I'll be fine doing so back at the condo."

"Kendra?" he asked, questioning if she was telling him the truth or not.

She looked at her watch.

"Maybe we could have stayed a little longer until I'm tired enough to go home and get right to sleep. I need tomorrow to hurry up and get here," she joked as they got in the car and rested back on the leather seating.

"I'm not tired either. How about, we walk off this dinner."

"Walk? Where? I'm in heels."

"I have the perfect place, if you're up for it. You won't need shoes."

"You sure? I saw you watching the time too. You were just as anxious as I am. You were calculating rushing to change and get back to them. Both of us need to relax and chill. There isn't a better place for them to be than at the hospital. You've got a guy posted to be sure any media doesn't try and sneak pictures of the boys."

"I'm sure. If you're up to it?"

"I am. It's a beautiful night. I'm assuming you mean someplace outdoors?"

"Oh, I'm talking about one of the most beautiful sights in the world."

Callum told the driver to take them to the resort.

"This time of night?"

"Relax. We'll be there shortly."

Callum followed his own directive as soon as he saw Kendra lean back. She shifted a few times and then he saw he whole body calm. That's what he was hoping for.

As the car made its way with old R&B playing through the speakers, a familiar song had he and Kendra sitting straight up, interrupting the quiet moment. It was the sound of Marvin Gaye and Tammi Terrell singing the words to the song that Callum knew stirred up old memories of a better time in their relationship. With her now, he felt the friendship. He missed the time when they were lovers. He turned his head to the left and Kendra was already looking at him with her eyes wide and as bright as the daytime sun. Awareness flared in her eyes. There was a time when this song came on that they would sing it to each other, solidifying what was growing between them. He was remembering those happy, loving, sweet and sexy times with her. From the way she was looking at him, she remembered them all too.

"Some coincidence, huh?" she asked.

"*You're all...I need*," Callum quickly sang and then stopped.

The car pulled up to the entrance of the locked gate to the resort. In light traffic, they had arrived quickly. The driver rolled down his window and Callum's. When the guards saw who it was, they were waved through. He gave the driver directions to turn toward the beach. There was still a lot to be done, but the beach was there. The view from the apartment he was staying in was a view he loved seeing every night. He couldn't wait to show it to Kendra from the edge of the ocean.

"The resort?" Kendra asked.

"More than the resort; the beach. There is a short walk and then we can take off our shoes. Giles, please stay on standby until we take Ms. Grimes home," Callum said to the driver.

"You got it, sir. I'll be near the gate. Just text when you're ready and I'll be right here."

Callum exited and helped Kendra out.

When the car pulled away, Callum reached for Kendra's hand and hoped that she wouldn't pull away. When she held tight to his hand, they headed toward the beach.

"Wow. We're not even on the sand yet and I can see why you chose this place. The ocean is gorgeous and as still as a statue. Is it always this quiet on the water?"

"Not all of the time, but when it is, it's a sight *and* sound worth taking in. Here, lift your foot and hand me your shoes. I'll carry them. Wait until you feel the sand under your feet. Some beaches you go to and the sand can be sort of abrasive. This sand is like walking on butter; not that you've actually done that to determine the difference. I think you'll love it."

"I already love everything I see."

Kendra laughed as he tried to juggle holding both their shoes.

"Including me carrying your shoes?"

"That most of all. You know, we've been to Hawaii a few times when we used to date or whatever we were doing."

"We were dating. You had it right. Don't try to diminish what that was. Yes, I messed up but when we came to Hawaii and spent time together, we were dating. That was when I finally learned how to relax and not think about work. That was because of you."

Callum escorted her to the beach and watched her face when she discovered he was telling the truth about how soft the sand was.

"I wasn't trying to talk down our time together. I couldn't. I have two amazing little boys who are a result of our time together. There was nothing bad about that time until there was that one time."

"I know. I wish I could go back."

Callum took Kendra's arm and linked it with his as they walked.

"And what? Change things? If only that were possible. We can't. We can move forward as parents. I think we're doing a great job of that. What are these large constructed boxes for? They are huge."

"They are the spots for the cabanas. They had to be measured out to make sure they weren't too close together. They're private all-night stay accommodations for guests who want a quiet romantic night looking up at the stars and enjoying the peacefulness of the ocean."

"And...*Making love*? Can they do that here?"

"If they want to, yes. We have rules about that, but yes, they can. There will be security around the clock. Each cabana will have secure walls, curtains for when they want to lower the walls. There are covers, a round, heart-shaped or large double king-size bed, controlled fire pits and all the pleasantries a loving couple would want. This resort is all about love, rekindling passion, new passion and new adventures for all guests. Everything about *Quiet Whisper* will speak of love. Now, don't get me wrong. We're not only marketing to couples. We will have a dynamic night life for singles as well. Everything we offer for couples, we cater to singles as well. Just no kids on this side."

"I remember going to *Secret Whisper* with you once. That's where this dream started. I remember how exciting that place was. Is *Silent Whisper* the same? I didn't have a chance to go there."

Callum stopped walking and turned to face her.

"If I invited you to *Silent Whisper* with me, would you go? I know I'm asking a lot. I don't quite know what I'm doing or trying to say. So much has transpired. I can't lie and say because you left me, I stopped caring about you or stopped being in love with you. I get it. I didn't say it. I also didn't act like it, but it's the truth. I have missed you. I've missed us having nights like tonight. It's extra special now because at the end of this, I also get to love on the two miracles you gave me. I know this isn't the right time, but I would like to know if there is a possibility that there could ever be an us again. These couple of months of you being here and me being able to see you every day, I hate that I tossed so much away."

"Callum, was it the sex? Did I not please you?"

"No, baby. No way. Is that what you've been thinking all this time? You think that you aren't and weren't enough to satisfy me? You were and are enough and then some. 1 was stupid. What I did had nothing to do with you not being enough. I knew it then. I really know it now because I screwed up and lost you. I am no different than any other guy out here making dumb moves like that because we think we can. I won't make up an excuse. My mother called me a bone-head."

"Your mother knows what happened?"

"Yes. She really likes you. She berated me for weeks for being average and not superior like she raised me. She reminded me that average men think with the wrong head. That always leads to trouble. Superior men know what can happen if they don't listen to the correct head."

"Were you acting on feelings for Tessa?"

"I never had any feelings her. I didn't know what you really meant to me until you left me. I wish you would let us try again."

"For the boys?"

Callum dropped the shoes and captured her face in his hands. He needed her to hear and see his heart in his words.

"Them and you. I would be lying if I didn't say that they have something to do with it. Before them, there was you. I tried to reach out to you for months after you left me. I've always wanted you back. That part has nothing to do with the boys. I felt that way before I knew they existed. I think I've come a long way to being the man who has learned a big lesson when it comes to the heart of a woman. I messed over yours and I'm sorry. For a long time, I've wanted to tell you that I love you. I did then. I do now. As our song says, you're all I need to get by. I'm heading toward completion and contentment in my life. That's not a bad thing. It is without you. No answer right now. We have enough on our plate. I'm hoping you will be open to it when life slows down. A kiss?"

He asked because they were in a place that was the most romantic spot in the world. There was no better person to share this space on this night with than her. She nodded and he didn't wait for a change of heart.

Callum kept his eyes focused on Kendra's when he touched his lips to hers. She tasted all kinds of sweet and sexy. When he felt her hands slide up to his chest, he deepened their connection when she invited him by slowly opening her mouth, allowing their tongues to get reacquainted. There was no rushing; no level of desperation of this being the last time. It was love, all love and complete desire. For him, the avid thirst he always held for her took his need higher. Pulling her close to him and loving the feel of her soft body against him had his body doing a happy dance. Under the full moon-lit sky, he poured his promise of never letting her down again into the kiss.

When they slowly pulled away, Kendra whispered something. He was still dizzy from the aromatic kiss that he didn't hear her. His mind was still doing flips of excitement that he was holding her in his arms.

"Baby?" he asked.

Kendra opened her eyes wider. To him, they looked heavy with an amatory haze.

"More," she said softly.

Callum smiled wide and moved in to feast on her lips again. If he was nothing, he was a man who had no problem dishing out satisfaction on her demand.

They stood like that right at the edge of the ocean, kissing like two star-crossed lovers. Time stood still as love and longing encased them. Several minutes passed when he noticed her thoroughly kissed, puckered lips. That was when he knew there was more to be had. There would be tonight if he didn't stop. He was prepared to lay her down on the sand and love her until the moon went away and it was replaced by the sun.

"I'd better get you home. I know you can feel me against you. When my thirst is evident, you know what that means. Whatever you decide about us, know that I'm here. I always will be. Ready to go?" he asked.

Callum reached for their shoes before reaching for her hand. Kendra didn't extend hers as she had done when they first arrived. He looked into her eyes to try and read them.

"I'm not."

"You want to stay longer? We can do that. It's a beautiful night."

"That's not what I meant."

Using the brightly lit moon, he searched her face again. Then he saw it. He knew.

"My place or yours."

Kendra smiled up at him and this time, she took his free hand in hers.

"Yours is closer. I think your driver would get a show if we had to wait to get to mine."

# 6

Kendra has so many questions for herself as she and Callum took their time walking to his apartment. She wasn't nervous or hesitant about what her request meant for them beyond tonight. What she did want was to feel Callum loving her the way she'd thought about for all the months they were apart.

They reached his apartment. He opened the door and moved so that she could move inside ahead of him. The moment she stepped inside, the lights came on, illuminating the open space all around them. She was surprised at the size. It was bigger than it appeared to be from the outside.

"This is nice. Are all of the guest resort rooms like this?"

"Most of them are. This side has been completed for a while. We did renovations to this part of the resort that was already standing when we purchased it. Everything here is brand new. My favorite feature is the large round bed out on the deck. This is a staple at all of our resorts. When we looked at the reviews for *Secret Whisper*, most guests said that one of the highlights of their stay was the comfortable bed out on the deck. The beds in the suites are now king size instead of queen. The showers are glass-enclosed and there are new his and her sinks in the extra-large bathroom. The living space here isn't a part of all the suites. Some also have more than one bedroom. I didn't need anything bigger than what I have."

"Is that because me being in your condo is temporary and

you'll eventually have your place back? I know you miss being in your own space."

"Baby, I would give it up a million times for you. I hope you can stop seeing it as my place, but as your place also."

When Callum opened his arms to her, Kendra sat her bag on the table next to the door and walked into his embrace.

"Are you sure?"

"Of?"

"This. I mean, I know you and your appetite. Are you doing this because I said, more?"

He didn't reply right away. Her heartbeat sped up to a fearful rate, unsure of whether his immediate silence meant something good or something bad.

"Pinch me," he finally said.

"What?"

"You heard me. Pinch me."

"Is that some sort of kinky thing?" she joked.

"You know me well. I'm not foreign to kinky anything, especially when it comes to pleasing you. I want you to pinch me so that you are clear that I am real and so is my thirst for you. You saying more reinforced the yearning I've had for you since forever. My body has been thumping like crazy for you. Then when I saw you open that door to me when I picked you up, my raging hormones went crazy. I would do any and everything for you. That includes soothing every itch you have. I, too, am in need of a scratch. You should always assume that I'm sure when it comes to you. The question is, are you sure?"

Kendra knew that being sure wasn't her issue. It was once they ventured into this territory again, could she trust that he won't hurt her again. Even if they don't define anything between them, her love for him still reigned strong in her heart. Relationship or not, she wasn't sure she could give herself to him without a doubt about the future.

"I want to feel. I want to feel all of you all over me and me all over you. I'm sure of that."

With Callum gazing into her eyes, Kendra saw a mirror of the fierce, fiery desire that glittered and sparkled with need that forged powerfully through her body. She needed him to remove all of the preoccupation she had about their past. The here and now was the priority.

To show him what she truly craved, she rose up as high as she could and placed her head between his chin and his chest. When his head rose slightly, she heard the hitch in his throat the second her lips touched his neck in a soft yet prevailing kiss. She turned her head so that she could move her mouth around his neck, planting kiss after kiss with closed and opened mouth delivery. Adding her tongue to the naughty affectionate move, the hum that cascaded from his throat encouraged her further.

Her hands went to where both were rested on either side of his hip to one moving down the center of his body. She moaned out her pleasure when she found him already steely hard, long and very thick. She shuddered when that part of him throbbed against her hand. One thing about Callum was that he was blessed when it came to his manhood and what he knew he could do with it. Pure satisfaction was in her immediate future. Her fingers caressed him through his pants.

"Tease," Callum whispered against her lips when he held her head in place so that he could plunder her mouth. He tilted her head to gain more access to her mouth. His soft lingering kisses turned feverish and hot with intense euphoria.

"Mmm, you like that. What's under my hand is telling me so," she said into his mouth.

He continued his plundering of her mouth again and again, going deeper and deeper while also driving the essence of pheromones escaping their bodies to encompass them in a haze of romantic possessiveness.

She willingly into his arms when he lifted her and moved them over to the bed. When he released her, placing her feet on the floor with her back to him, the most incredible sight was before her. Callum had the curtains at the sliding glass door opened all the way. There was nothing blocking her view of the full moon and beautifully starry night. The tantalizing atmosphere had her feeling the sexiest she's ever experienced. That's saying a lot considering Callum had been a master at setting an air of potent energy.

"This moon shining on you illuminates all of the beauty that you are," Callum said against her neck.

She felt his hands swipe down the sides of her body where he gathered her dress in his hands. Raising it, along with her arms, he removed the dress from her body, leaving her standing in front of him in a pair of high-cut black lace panties and a strapless, lace demi-bra. She held her breath as his teeth nibbled on her shoulder, first one side and then the other; his hands covering her breasts. When his fingers slipped inside of the cups of her bra, she knew that any minute she would fall in a heap at his feet. Her body was screaming for release. It had been all night. To show him, she leaned back into his body, moving her hips in a circular manner.

"Please," she said on a slight, yet desperate request.

"I know. You want release. Baby, we are not in a rush. We have as much time as you need to get as many releases as your body can stand in one night," Callum said, chuckling sexily against her neck.

Reaching behind her, he released her bra. When his bare hands caressed her breasts this time, they ached out of sheer pleasure and demand to give her hard, pebbled tips the attention they needed.

With one hand slowly caressing from one breast over to the other, he slid one hand down her body and behind the lace barrier of her panties to that place that was screaming for him to touch, to kiss, to love. His fingers caressed the outside of her womanhood, moving his digits around and around; her hips gliding back and forth across them.

"I need…"

"Baby, I know exactly what you need. Your need is all over my hand. I got you. Feel."

"Yes," she expressed lasciviously again and again.

Callum played there, stirring up all the feels that were quickly sending her body and mind into the stratosphere of ecstatic bursts of lust.

Her hips gyrated with a happy climb to a surging explosion as his hands move with the intent of driving her mad with craving for the wave of ecstasy that was chasing after every part of her body.

Callum held her close to his body, rubbing his hardness against her back to remind her that there was more to come. She had no need to prolong the inevitable.

"Let go, baby," he said against her neck where he captured her skin between his teeth and held on.

With his mouth on her neck, his hand caressing her breasts and a hand stroking her between her legs, she caved as her vaginal walls gripped his fingers as they slid in and out of her. Her body and mind let go as she rode the waves of pleasure that carried her body up, up and away to a blissful place of pure delight. Her body fed from his touch, his kiss, his caress. Her mouth screamed as a tingling warmth shot through her limbs. The sexy feeling went on and on. When her climax began to release her, gradually slowing down the grinding of her hips, she let her head fall forward as she tried to breathe through the sheer insanity of the flurry of tantalizing zings that vigorously gripped her.

Callum turned her around and captured her lips, going at her mouth like a starving man. Then he did the sexiest move. He lifted his finger to his lips and wiped the essence from her body across them before slowly moving them into his mouth. His sexy eyes darkened and just like that, seeing him enjoying the taste of her had her ready for more. Her body was again experiencing a desperate want for another climatic moment. He then kissed her with a delicious opened mouth kiss, letting her taste her own body from his mouth. The moment was the most erotic scene that her brain had ever taken in.

No words were exchanged as he stopped to remove her panties from her body.

"You may have to go home panty-less because these are too wet to wear. That is not a bad thing," Callum rising and taking her body with him.

He loving laid her down across the bed while he quickly removed his clothes. She tried to reach for that part of him that pointed in her direction. Callum wasn't having that at all.

"If I let you touch me, this will be over before I even get inside of you. What I need, and by the looks of you, what you need as well, is me inside of you."

"Yes. Please," Kendra slurred out, still encased in the sexual afterglow of her release.

She could still feel small shudders rocking her to her core when Callum moved above her, moving his mouth over her breasts. He gave each equal attention, pulling on her nipples with his teeth allowing a sizzling sensation to ready her body even more for him.

He slipped his hands under her hips. She opened her

trembling legs as her body begged for him. She followed his gaze to that area where he slowly connected their bodies in a slow, erotic move that had her body on the brink of desperation for another orgasm. With one long surge, Callum entered her body and began to move with one power stroke after another. He moved her legs until they lightly encircled her body as thankful notions quietly screamed out for all of him. The all-consuming kiss that clawed at all of her senses had her unable to decide what pleasure point on her body she wanted to focus on the most. There wasn't one because Callum was doing what she had begged him for. He was letting her feel him all over and in her. They bucked and rocked together. Each stroke went deeper and more penetrating than the last. Her body was greedy. Her hips met Callum's hips stroke for stroke. She gave to him as much as he was giving to her. She was wholly filled with passion.

His grunts and small growls took them higher and faster just the way she loved. He kissed her with a flurry of hard kisses that again sent her into a dizzying, sexual jerk when her body let go again with one hell of an orgasm searing through every part of her. As she flailed uncontrollably through her release, she heard Callum's primitive, animalist grown consume him. Callum's grip on her hips tightened as she locked her legs behind his body and happily took every hard surge into her body. His strokes moved them across the bed until her head reached the other side, almost off the edge of the bed. He held her close as she continued to respond with her hips giving him more and more. She clawed at his back while Callum leaned up and back and roared like a lion. He was a true and fierce Leo for sure. His body shuddered again and again. He brought his mouth down on her hard, kissing her with determined strokes of his tongue against hers, loving her with a need that reminded her that he said he had a thirst for her and only her. If he never proved that again, he did tonight.

Their bodies began to relax from the throes of the potent aphrodisiac sensations that flowed through them moments ago. She held onto him, caressing his sweat-covered back until his shivers of delight lessened.

"What...the...hell...was...that?" Callum stuttered out. "I think I'm having a heart attack," he jested. "Or maybe, just maybe, this is love."

Kendra couldn't speak. His loving had brought tears to her eyes. She was afraid that if she opened her mouth to speak, she would cry from the pleasure that he rained down on her body. He kissed her sweetly. He tasted like the magic of satisfaction that she sought when they entered the room. She held his body close to hers as his body continued to throb inside of hers. She never wanted to lose this closeness or any of the feelings she experienced this night.

"I love you," she said against his face.

"I love you, too, baby. You are an unquenchable thirst."

**

Callum jumped up out of bed a little disoriented. His body's clock signaled him that he was oversleeping. Checking his phone, it was close to three in the morning. He looked back to the bed where Kendra was deep in sleep. He hated waking her even for a second. He wasn't sure she'd gotten sleep this good since she arrived. He reached for his phone to get a look at the boys. He smiled seeing that both were sound asleep. In the bed next to the crib, he could see his cousin just as sound asleep as they were. His plan to spend the night at the hospital could be put aside. As long as Kendra was okay with that, he would be as well.

Slipping on his boxers, he slid back into bed, snuggling up to Kendra's back. He kissed her shoulder while his hand slid beneath the thin blanket to caress her hip.

"Baby? Kendra?"

He moved a little when she did exactly what he had done. Kendra hopped up so fast he raised his hands to let her know she was in a safe space.

"The boys!" she shouted.

Callum handed her his phone so that she could see that they were okay.

"They're fine. I woke up the same way you just did. We were both deep in sleep. I got right up and reached for my phone."

"I'm glad you installed that camera. That was a brilliant idea."

"It was. I wish I had thought of it earlier. They're good. Come back to bed. I wouldn't have disturbed you but I didn't know if you wanted to spend the night here. Do you want me to take you to the condo or to the hospital?"

"What time is it?"

"A little after three in the morning."

"This will be our only night before they come home. I don't want to get up. This bed is comfortable. Even more so because I was in your arms. Do you mind if I stay here with you tonight? I don't even know if my legs will carry me," she said snuggling up to him.

"Intense, huh? Was I too intense?"

"With me? Never. I love how you put all of yourself into making love. I felt you all over. It wasn't too much of anything. You were exactly what I needed. I hope it was that way for you too. It's been a long time for us."

"For me, too long."

"Too long with me or too long with...never mind. I shouldn't have. That was about to be a dumb question."

Callum kissed her lips and lingered there until she moaned

her pleasure against his lips. When her hand went lower under the blanket, he reached for her hand and smiled against her lips.

"There are no dumb questions. I know what you were about to ask. Just to be clear, I haven't been with anyone since that night. I know it wasn't with you, but no one since then. Thirsting for you means only you for me."

"Callum, you don't have to say that. I know how you enjoy the pleasures of a woman's body."

"It's the truth. There hasn't been anyone at all. Couldn't you tell by how deeply I loved you tonight that I had a lot of sexual tension built up in me."

"Why did you move my hand just now? We're woke and I can tell you're more than ready. And you have clothes on."

"I didn't know if I needed to get dressed to take you home or to go to the hospital. I just slipped them on. Before I get fully dressed, I figured I would see if getting dressed was necessary."

"It's not, but getting undressed again?"

"No. Before you question, I just said no to sex. Can you believe that? I can't either."

Kendra couldn't believe it. There has never been a time that they were together that he didn't want to make love to her.

"I'm shocked."

"And don't start putting a million little questions of doubt in your head. You and I could both use more sleep. I'm going to set the alarm on my phone to get us up at eight. If we get up earlier, that's fine. I am hoping we will both stay in this bed until then and focus on sleeping. We'll get up so that I can get you home to get dressed. We'll grab something to eat and then go pick up our boys who are finally coming home."

Kendra sat up and turned to face him.

"Is it wrong that I'm a little bit nervous? What if something goes wrong? What if you're here and I'm there with them?"

"I'm not going anywhere. I already have a rollout bed that I'm going to put in their room. I'll be there anytime you want and need. We're taking care of them together. You're going to get sick of me because I'll be there so much. We got this. Come on back down here and get some sleep. No more worries. Good dreams. Happy thoughts only."

She did as he asked. When he pulled her close, she stayed that way; holding onto him as tight as she could. Her last thought before she slipped into slumber was that they had wasted a lot of time getting to this moment. This felt good; it felt right. It felt like she could be like this with him forever. Her fear was that forever for them could come with too many uncertainties. Everything with Callum felt wonderful but was it really a true reality?

# 7

Callum was all smiles as he walked out of the hospital with his sons for the first time. Kendra was capturing the moment on live video chat for all of the family to see them leaving the hospital and happy about it. He could hear his and her family cheering through Kendra's phone as they all watched Finn and Liam, after months of surgeries and tests, go home for the first time since their ordeal began months ago back in Las Vegas.

"They're looking good!" Tellum yelled.

"Yes!" Cheyenne added.

"Look at my nephews!" Byrum cheered.

"I see you, little fellas," Keiko added.

"Look at our babies," Felicia and Dennis said together.

"Tony, can you see them?" Melissa asked.

She was in Las Vegas while he was on the road with his team.

"I do and I plan to see them soon in person in a week when I fly to Hawaii."

"I can't wait to hold them," Amelia declared.

"Not before me," TJ exclaimed.

Everyone was present and accounted for.

Callum moved toward the back of the black Cadillac Escalade truck sitting in front of the hospital. They had security around to shield any view of their sons from cameras from those hoping to get a first look at the twins who have been in the news lately along with their celebrity parents. Callum was happy that they were strategic in how they would introduce their sons to the world. There had been media scoping out the hospital for months.

He first lifted up Finn to secure him in the back. He could still hear his family all trying to talk at the same time, throwing out tons of questions that Kendra was doing her best to answer.

"Everybody, I promise I will connect us again after we get the boys home. I can answer all of your questions. It's sort of hard to do with them coming at me seven at a time," Kendra relayed and then blew kisses to all of them.

"Y'all heard her. We can't get them settled in the truck and respond to a million questions," Callum noted.

"That truck looks new," Tellum said.

"It is. I had it delivered this morning. It's Kendra's," he exclaimed.

He turned his head just as realization hit her.

"What? You bought me a truck? A big one at that. Really?"

"I did. You need privacy and space to travel them around in. I have a driver ready to go anytime you need or drive it yourself; whatever you want. In fact, here are the keys. You can drive us the few blocks to the condo."

"Dada."

There was silence. Did his ears hear him. Callum looked at Finn who was reaching for him.

"You said, Dada. Did y'all hear that? Finn said, Dada. I know I heard it."

"We didn't hear anything," Byrum said loudly.

"Dada."

Callum was not hearing things. His son was looking at him and calling his name. This is a moment never to be forgotten.

That time it was Liam when he picked him up to carry him around to the other side of the truck now that Finn was security locked in.

"Yes! I know y'all heard that."

"Okay, I heard it that time. The boys both said, Dada. Hell, I thought that they would say Mama first. I told y'all them boys love their daddy," Kendra laughed.

"Yeah, we did hear it that time. Music to our ears," Felicia said. "Your father and I will be there in about a week. Let me know if you need anything before then. Nothing is too small or too big, Kendra. I'm saying this to you because Callum won't listen. He'll go out and purchase the world for them."

"You're right, mom. Callum, don't you dare to that," Byrum hollered.

"Whatever. Finn, Liam, say bye, bye to everybody until later," Callum said.

When their little hands opened and closed as Kendra held the screen up for everyone to see them, they all once again cheered. The loud booming sound of that quickly stunned the boys, who then laughed with everyone else.

"We have to go. We should be home shortly. Give us time to get the heart monitors all set up before y'all start calling every hour," Kendra explained.

"I've sent some prepared food to the condo. There should be enough for lunch and dinner for the next few days. Callum can make you breakfast," Felicia said.

"I got it, mom. Thanks for that," he said.

"We love you!" Kendra said before ending the video chat.

"That was a lot," Callum said as he climbed in the truck and sat between Liam and Finn. "Fellas, we got this. We're staying in for the rest of the day, so today and tomorrow, we're good," Callum said to the five security guys.

One helped Kendra into the driver's side of the truck as another helped the nursing staff load up a few large bags into the back of the truck.

With everyone secured, Kendra pulled out into traffic.

"Are you nervous with them coming home? It's really, real, isn't it?" she asked.

Callum checked each heart monitor that was connected to the boys. He looked at all of the signals the doctors told him to watch for.

"Nervous and so freaking happy!"

He yawned and Kendra laughed and beamed at him in the rearview mirror.

"Tired?" she asked.

"You're not? All those plans of getting as much sleep as we could last night didn't actually happen."

"Well, you are the one who kept reaching for me throughout the night."

"It's your fault I couldn't get enough of you. I'm good though. We have to work on sleep patterns now that they're home. Besides, I'll be off for the next few weeks. I know having twins isn't an easy walk in the part. I don't care if I don't get a lot of sleep. I'm already planning to spend my days and nights just watching them sleep. Our two little chubby checkers. Dada?" he asked both boys.

They clapped at him, still reaching for him to pick them up.

"It's the potatoes and green beans all mashed up that's got our boys already looking like linebackers. For what they've been through, that's a good thing."

As Kendra drove, Callum reached out and let each son grab ahold of one of his fingers. They loved having him and Kendra close enough to touch. He had to admit that their affection was a major part of his day. He leaned back on the seat and kept his eyes on her. He was remembering the night before.

After their first love session, both had fallen asleep, only to rise up with awareness of what had transpired. It was a love session that had been a long wait; at least for him.

"Don't forget the list of things you need from the store. I can have someone go pick up everything or we can have the ordered delivered. I know we were going to do that this morning, but we ran out of time."

"Oh? *We* ran out of time? I was all set to leave the resort on time this morning. It was you who wouldn't let me shower alone. That led to sex in the shower. Oh, then sex after the shower, which led to another shower where I had to lock the sliding door to the bathroom to keep you out."

"Yeah, but then you made me suffer by watching you shower through the glass window between the shower and the bed. Tease," he said, for the second time.

She winked at him.

"Like you tell me, I got you."

"Yes, you do. You've got me sprung wide open, Kendra."

"Before I pull into the condo garage, do you need to stop at the resort to get anything? You're staying with us, right?"

"Baby, where else am I going to go? No, I don't need to get anything. Most of my things are still at the condo. I'd rather get them home and settled. It will be nap time soon. The nurse said they've been up all morning with no nap. A good bath and lunch will relax them."

Callum knew that if it were up to him, he would never leave them for any reason. This was his life. The scene before him of his sons babbling about something and him and Kendra bonding was what he needed. What he had to do was convince Kendra that they were more than just parents who engaged in sexual romps. Now that they've gotten that first night of love making out of their systems, he was planning for much more. *Quiet Whisper*, though not actually open for guests yet had been the perfect setting for loving Kendra again like he'd dreamed about for months. The real her was so much better. He was understanding the hold the other two resorts had on his brothers. They had either discovered or rediscovered love at them. He was in the midst of doing the same with Kendra in Hawaii.

"When we stopped this morning to let me change, I laid out onesies to put them in for their first day home. They are cute. I think they were from your mother. They have more outfits than me and you put together," Kendra said.

"There is so much love all around them. That's what got us through this time. It's all love. I think we still need to talk about us," Callum said as Kendra entered the garage and parked in one of his two private spaces.

"I know we do. Last night wasn't planned. We talked some before and after, but not the way we need to. There is a lot to iron out."

"You have questions?" he asked.

Callum knew the time would come when they would eventually have to talk about the breakup.

After she left Chicago that night without as much as a single word when she walked in on him and Tessa, they had never said another word to each other until she arrived in Hawaii. There was still so much left unsaid. It was that part of their history that they needed to deal with if they were ever going to move beyond that memory. He wanted to find a way to wipe it out of her head. Yes, he was that cocky Callum. He wasn't that person anymore; not for a long time. Not since he felt in his heart what his actions had done to her. He never wanted to hurt a woman or see a woman hurt the way in which he had done her.

"I do. I'm not sure I'm ready to hear the answers. We had no contact for over a year; nothing at all. Yes, we have the boys. Yes, I brought them here because they needed their father. I needed your help with them. We leaped right into focusing on them without really talking. Then we leaped back into bed together as if time hadn't been the elephant in the room."

Callum got out and took Liam out first. He was already falling asleep and whimpering because he couldn't get as comfortable as he wanted to. Liam was the fussy one when it came to fighting sleep.

Kendra closed the car door behind him as he went around to the other side to get Finn out. He paid close attention to the wires that connected each of them to a small monitor. The equipment would allow the hospital to check for any abnormal changes in their heart rhythms.

Kendra went to open the back of the truck.

"Leave that stuff. After I get them upstairs, I'll come back and get everything."

"Okay."

"We will talk, Kendra. I don't hold it against you that I've tried talking to you the whole time and you didn't want anything to do with me. I know and I understand. I've asked you for another chance. We made love all night and it was amazing. I also know that sex won't get us back on track. I wish that it could because we are great together. It's not a start or an answer. It's us needing that time together. There is still so much more to me and you."

Kendra locked the truck before they headed to the elevator. The ride up didn't lend to much conversation because Finn decided he wanted to have a conversation all the way up.

"Since the moment they recognized their own voices, they love the sound of them. Well, except for Liam who is already asleep. Hi, mommy's baby," Kendra said to Finn who waved his arms playfully in the air at her.

Callum watched the exchange between them. He was happy seeing how joyful the twins were. The doctors were concerned when they first arrived because they had little movement or interaction. They were also pretty small, even for twins. Getting them healthy had them felling and looking so much better. With that came a lot of crawling and attempts to stand and walk. The talking and sign language was an extra added bonus.

"These little sailor suits are cute. Are we doing the dressing alike thing with them? I see that they have the same outfit on but in two different colors."

"I want to dress them alike, but not exactly alike. I want them to have separate personalities without thinking they must dress alike. Thankfully, they aren't identical twins which makes it easy to tell them apart," she said.

"That's helpful considering they'll be in the same crib. I agree about similar but not the same in everything. There are so many decisions to be made as parents. I never thought about what it would take to be a parent."

"We didn't plan for them. We also didn't unplan for last night, you get that, right?"

Callum knew. What she is thinking had also crossed his mind.

"No condom. I know. I thought about that too. I'm not worried," he said.

"Because you think this won't happen? We have twins that say it's possible. I was on birth control when I got pregnant with them. I still am on it, more so to regulate my cycle, which you know has been a problem for me."

"I do know that. No. I'm not worried, because I love you. If you're pregnant, we'll figure that out just like we're figuring this out; together."

"Callum, you say that now."

"No, I'm saying that now and forever. Kendra, I don't have a problem if you were to get pregnant again. It's your body. I'm with you no matter what. I won't be upset about you having another baby by me. Would you be?"

While he waited for her to answer as they walked down the hall where she unlocked the door and moved for him to enter, he remembered waking up before her this morning and thinking about the lack of protection they had in place the three times he'd made love to her. He wasn't a man to love on any woman, other than her, without a condom. She had been the only woman who could say he'd ever done that. Going forward, he wouldn't risk it again. He just wanted her so bad the night before that his only thought was on loving her deeply and as often as her body could stand. He missed her more than his words, heart or body knew until he'd had her in his embrace again.

"I will say it this way; I love Finn and Liam and no, another baby wouldn't send me into a wild spin. I'm not planning on another baby, but I know how eager we were to be together last night. I don't want another unplanned pregnancy, especially with them being so young. If it happens as a result of last night, I would be just as happy about that baby as I am about the two we have. I wouldn't want to stifle any plans you have for your life. I never saw myself as a father. Now, I can't see myself as anything other than a father."

Callum walked into the family room and placed the boys in their seats on the large mat he'd put down on the floor this morning while he waited for her to get dressed.

"Since having the babies, I haven't thought much about my plans other than getting them healthy and being their mom. Like you, I didn't see myself as a mother, at least not this early. I figured in my thirties, late thirties. I wouldn't change anything. They came at a time when I needed something new and bright in my life. That's definitely our boys."

Callum nodded. He was with her on that.

"I'm going to get the rest of the things out of the truck. Do you need me to pick up anything before I come back up? There is a message on the intercom screen from the lobby attendant that there are boxes of sealed food that were delivered. That must be what my mother mentioned. I'll have those brought up, but not until I come back."

Kendra looked over at him and smiled with all of her teeth.

"Condoms, Callum. Get some," she said and sat down on the floor in front of now, two sleeping boys.

"I will pick up some. Anything else?" he asked and winked at her a few times.

"Let me rephrase that – get a *lot* of condoms."

Callum laughed out loud.

"Will I get to use any tonight?" he quipped.

"If we can get these two down for the night, you will absolutely get lucky. Oh, and bring me some chocolate."

"Peanut M&M's?"

"You know me so well."

"When I get back, there is a lot more that I'd like to know. Before we get too far, I want to know what the past year or so has been like since you left me. I care about what you went through after that night. I couldn't fix it then. I can't fix it now. I can hear you out. I also want to reassure you that nothing like that will ever happen again. I just need another chance. Think about that. I'll be back as fast as I can. I want to help bathe them. I love that time with them and you."

"I'll wait on you to get back for that. I am going to change them because somebody smells a little ripe! I can't tell which one," she said kissing both Liam and Finn again and again on their cheeks.

"Kiss them for me too," Callum said, turning toward the door. He stopped before he opened it and walked over to them.

He first kissed Finn's forehead and then Liam's. When Kendra looked over at him, he didn't go for her forehead. He went for a kiss on her lips that was more than a quick peck. He took her lips in a shamelessly wild, all-out sensual and deeply loving assault. He would never get enough of tasting her; all of her, especially her perfectly, kissable mouth.

He then rushed out to the truck. Before pulling off, he took out his phone and sent a text to both Tellum and Byrum.

*"Pray that I get my love with Kendra back."*

*"We got you brother,"* Tellum messaged.

*"Already on it,"* Byrum added.

Smiling, Callum pulled off so that he could quickly get back to his family.

# 8

Callum attempted to silence his team who were gathered around one of the *Quiet Whisper* resort conference room tables.

"Alright, alright. I can't hear everyone at the same time. Is this how the marketing meetings usually go? All of you pushing your opinions on each other at the same time? I don't hear a coordinating voice in the room. Tim, this is supposed to be your team. What am I listening to if it's not you pulling this together into one thought, one mind?"

Callum didn't mean for his words to come out so harsh, but he wasn't happy with everyone's pleas for his attention to what they each thought was best. He turned from all of their faces and turned to his Director of Marketing, Timothy Force.

"Sorry, Callum. I don't know what kind of time they're on today. I think everyone is excited to have you back in the office. We have an entire plan to put before you today."

"Sorry, boss," the team said around the room.

"Let's figure this out. I know I've been out of the office for three weeks. I hoped that my brothers and I were right in the teams that we selected to keep things moving ahead. I've been getting updates and even sat in on a few calls. I spoke with Tellum last night and he said the call with the marketing teams from *Secret Whisper* and *Silent Whisper* went well. With *Quiet Whisper* moving full speed ahead, I need the game plan coming together for promoting this place by itself while also working with the other teams to market all three resorts together. I saw the new draft website for this place and it's great. I wouldn't change a thing. Thanks, Omar, for sending me the specs for that."

"Sure. I'm glad you approve. Tellum and Byrum gave a little feedback, but pretty much liked it as is. I'll make a few tweaks from them and get this sent back to you all for a final look."

Callum nodded to Omar who was crucial in the online presence of all of their resorts. Having him in Hawaii was a must.

"I want to hear about where we are with the billboards. Where are we with the social media plans? What's going on with the giveaway drawings for the free stays? You guys have me for the next fifty minutes. My calendar is booked for the rest of the day with meetings. You've already wasted five minutes with this unruly back and forth."

"Tim is right. We're really happy to have you back. He's been doing a great job. We are in capable hands," Erica, another member on the team said.

Callum smiled to ease the tension in the room.

"I do want to take a moment to say thank you for all the baby gifts. You all didn't have to do that. Kendra and I are thankful."

"We can't wait to meet them. I know you all have been keeping them close since the social media hype ramped up. We're sorry about all the attention into your personal life. Any update on how information that personal about your sons got out?" Tim asked as he prepared the large screen at the end of the room for their presentation.

"Someone at the hospital leaked information about my son's medical issues," Callum explained.

Inside, he was still fuming when CMZ, a national media company released intimate knowledge and photos of him and

Kendra at the hospital. Thankfully, no one was able to get any footage of the boys. Still, information about their medical care was leaked to the media. After an investigator for the hospital and one he personally hired a week ago were able to talk to everyone who had been on the floor during Finn and Liam's stay, the culprit confessed and then apologized. He decided to let the hospital deal with the disciplinary action that resulted in the woman being fired. He didn't want any parts of what happened, though Kendra wanted the woman's head on a block.

One of the things he knew that came along with his celebrity as a business mogul, worth millions and her celebrity status as a professional women's basketball player was the public's interest in their lives. Some didn't care the lengths they had to go through to get information that they could sell to the highest bidder. One consequence was that the offender at the hospital had to donate the money they received for leaking the information. That seemed to be the hardest pill for the woman to swallow, even over losing her job.

"I hope they've been dealt with. That's awful. People have no boundaries," Tim said.

"Very true. There is extra security around them and Kendra, so we're good. Thanks for asking. Are we ready?" he asked.

Callum was hoping to take his mind off of the drama of the past two weeks. The high that he and Kendra were on was temporarily lessened when his brothers called to inform him of what they were hearing on social media.

He and Kendra had decided to step away from all things news related so that they could focus on their family. The boys were growing nicely and would hopefully soon be off of the heart monitors. Their checkups, both at the hospital and at home with doctor and nurse visits were going well.

Things with him and Kendra were still up in the air. They tried talking about what happened the night he'd cheated on her with Tessa. When they started talking about it, her first question was if that was his first time cheating. She also wanted to know if he'd been with Tessa more than once while they were together. He answered no to both questions. He also assured her that the only time he had been with someone else was during a four month span the first year they were together when they had broken up. She didn't know about that and was shocked to hear it. When he tried to explain what happened with Tessa, Kendra had shut down completely and didn't want to hear more. He gave her that and ended the conversation. He would try again. Until they could get through that, he wasn't sure their relationship could move forward.

Nothing, not even the unknown, had kept them from continuing the intimate part of their relationship. Over the three weeks since Finn and Liam had come home, a peace had settled over them. They balanced each other out when it came to the boys not always being on the same schedule, especially when it came to naps and going down for the night. They were discovering the monitors that were connected to them. A few days ago, a technician arrived and changed the connection from wired to wireless. They always kept some kind of shirt or undershirt on them to make sure they didn't touch or mess with the node that were attached to their chests.

"Callum, here is where we are with the rollout plan. We have secured billboard space in the largest cities around the country. Of course, there is a marketing plan for *Quiet Whisper* at all of your resorts, not just *Secret Whisper* and *Silent Whisper*. Hannah and I are traveling to all of the resorts over the next four months to see the covered billboards go up. We're prepared to unveil each one on the same day once we're ready. There is a full media blitz in the making. It's going to be huge. The buzz about this place has thousands of people asking about attending the unveilings. The lottery here on Hawaii will launch in a few months. There will be a chance for fifteen free weekend stays that can be used within a year of our grand opening. There are radio and television ads. Of course, all social media platforms will be flooded. We have celebrities who are reaching out to us daily to inquire about being spokespeople for the resorts. They love what others have been able to achieve by doing that for your other resorts. The marketing for the grand opening will be a large media barrage on all major networks because we have some of the biggest talents in television, movies and music being a part of the first month of the launch. Each room at all of the resorts will have marketing materials for *Quiet Whisper* in them."

A member of his team handed him an iPad that showed him a 3-D image of the resort and what it will look like when it's done. He loved it all.

"This is done using AI?" he asked.

"Absolutely. That's the way to go with everything. We will also reach out to frequent guests of our other resorts to compliment them for a three-night, four-day stay here. They will all get a special box that will have this video along with other gifts for their stay. We're asking that they unpack their boxes on their social media platforms to increase the buzz. To be honest, boss, even if we do nothing, we are already booked for well over a year for the rooms we know will be available for both the adult-only side and the family side. Word of mouth so far has been crazy. I will say, and I apologize for connecting this, but the recent stories about your sons and Kendra have had our booking lines ringing off the hook. People are even walking up to the gates and asking for information on how they can book and whether or not you and Kendra will have your children here for photo opportunities."

Callum looked up, raising one eye brow higher than the other.

"You already know the answer to that. Let's keep them guessing, but no, there will be no photos with my family," he explained.

"We already know, boss. We are almost a year out from opening and yet people want to book and pay to lock in their vacation stays now. The interior designer, Loren Knight, is doing this huge interview on Tamron Hall, The Jennifer Hudson Show and a few other big newsworthy shows. She's also the spotlight in the next *Essence* spread with the story about how her design company has grown into a multi-million-dollar business over the past ten years. She wanted us to know that on each of her appearances, including the *Essence* spread, she mentions the work she's done on all of the resorts."

"That's great. Her designs are award-winning. We're lucky to have her onboard," Callum interjected.

"That's an even larger marketing push. She's going to send some videos and photos our way if you would like to use them. She said she's sending them at no cost. She and her husband, Michael, love the partnership that has been created between them and the Blackstone family. The growth on both sides is due to your work together," Tim explained.

Callum clapped loudly.

"Amazing work guys. Here, I was prepared to chop a few heads when I walked in. Outstanding work. Please send a few dozen roses to Loren to thank her for always being in our corner. She's right – the partnership with her company and that of her husband and his two friends, Tyrone and Duron, through their architecture firm has been a major blessing. I believe there are people from her team coming in this week to finish up the event hall. That has to be the first area, besides the hotel rooms above it, that we have ready because of Byrum's upcoming wedding in a few months. Are we ready? This is our first event to show what we have. We are allowing some media for that so that we can get first glimpses of the accommodations in the public eye," he asked.

The closer they get to the wedding, and what will come after that when they eventually open, had Callum on a natural high. He thought things would be derailed because he had to turn his attention to his family. His brothers did what brothers do. They stepped in where he needed them.

"We are more than ready. Loren's team was here two weeks ago to make sure the suites above the event center are ready. Yes, they're returning again in a week. Byrum and Keiko let us know that they would need one hundred and seventy-five rooms. Sharon and I will do the final walkthrough two weeks before the wedding since some of your family will be here one week before the nuptials. We are ready. Trust me, no one in this room is interested in letting you down. You personally hand-selected each team member either from the Detroit office or from right here in Honolulu. We are a well-oiled machine, for sure. With the time we have left, I have about ten minutes more of a presentation with the remaining time being left for questions you may have that we will answer."

"Callum's next meeting will start thirty minutes after this meeting ends, so if you can wrap up on time, that will give him a few minutes to prepare for the updates on the restaurants."

Callum nodded to one of his executive assistants, Leslie, who along with two others, kept his life on track around the office.

"I'm also flying out of town on business in a little over a week. Before I leave, my brothers will both be here for two days. I'd like to meet with every team while they are here. Just like you gave me this update, I'd like the same for them. We'll patch in the mirrored teams at all of the other resorts so that we can talk about plans for each for the next five years."

"I've got all of this noted, Callum. I'll connect with each of your brothers' assistants to be sure we're all on the same page," Leslie said.

"Great. Tim, you've got about, ten minutes. Let's go."

Callum leaned back with a level of excitement he's been living on for months now. Not only was he back on track with the resort, but he was also hoping for the same for his personal life. He knew that he was able to convince Kendra to stay until the boys healed enough to travel. That time was going to one day come up. He didn't know what he was going to do. If he was going to reunite them as one, he had to show her that he was ready for her. They were growing closer but still, something was eating away at him. Kendra, who he was drawn to because of her confidence, was shying away from that and he didn't know why. Was she still not ready to trust him? Something was telling him that he'd hit the nail on the head. How to fix that, he didn't have a clue.

# 9

Kendra was already smiling when she knocked of Callum's opened office door. When he looked up and saw her and then his eyes landed on the double stroller she was pushing, he leaped up and hurried around his desk. He first kissed her, slowing down his approach in order to slow down the kiss. One thing about him was that he didn't care who was present around him. He was going to kiss her like he hadn't seen her in months. She loved any feel of his lips on her. When he was finished loving on her, he leaned down to the excitement of their two little ones, Finn dressed in blue denim shorts and a white shirt with little white sneakers on his feet to Liam dressed in black denim shorts, white shirt and white sneakers. Both had little matching hats, one with the number one and the other with the number two on it. They shrieked with joy the moment they saw him. Their little toothy grins made his day, as usual. Kendra saw the brightest beam on Callum's face.

"To say they are happy to see daddy would not give justice to the smiles on their faces. They've been singing for you all morning, so I thought I would come by and say hello."

"I'm glad you did. The team has been asking about meeting them since I arrived this morning. I didn't know you were coming through. As you can see, I'm happy that you did. It's good you're out too," he said looking to the two men on the security team who stood at the door of the entrance to the office.

"I called your guys to see if they were available today. I wanted to take them to the park just to sit there, not to get out and play. They are not ready for that. They're cutting more teeth. This morning after you left was rough. Those refrigerated teething toys I ordered really worked. Remind me to never leave home without them."

"How was getting them in the car without me?"

Kendra gave him a thumbs up as he maneuvered holding both boys in his arms. He had to hold them tight as they bounced around for what they are used to as play time anytime he picked them up. They didn't care that he was at work. Neither did he.

"The nanny was there to help me carry them down. You carry both carriers at the same time with no problem. The way they are eating, they are getting heavy. I forgot to take the stroller out of the truck after we came in from the appointment with the doctor yesterday. We usually roll them in it to the condo, but you carried them yesterday. Slipped my mind because I wasn't planning to come out today."

"From now on, I'll make sure it doesn't stay in the back of the truck. I can tell they are getting heavier now that they are eating a lot better. You look amazing, baby."

Kendra shyly smiled remembering her desire to entice Callum with the yellow striped skirt and matching solid yellow top. She wore flat sandals, a rarity for her, since she had to handle both boys. She was already missing her high heels.

"Thank you. Listen, I need to talk to you. I know you have work to do since your last day back in the office all day is today. I don't want to interrupt."

Kendra had been thinking on something for a few days. She wasn't sure how to broach the subject with him. She got a call earlier that had her excited, up and out to see him. This wasn't a phone conversation.

"I have all the time in the world for you."

Kendra moved further into the office and sat on the long brown leather sofa. Callum moved behind his desk and sat as he smiled and made faces at Liam and Finn that had them laughing out loud at his antics.

"My agent received a request about me last week. She was hesitant about reaching out since I don't play ball anymore. I'm still retaining her as my agent."

"Okay."

She nervously wrung her hands together.

"They want you back on the team?"

"No, not that. They know I'm not interested in that, at least not any time soon. I may never. I don't know because I haven't thought about that. She's been getting requests for a photo spread of us with the boys from *People Magazine*. They want an exclusive before others get images of Finn and Liam. I wanted to run this by you because the request was for the four of us, not just me and the boys. I didn't know what image you wanted to put out of us, if any at all. I'm not saying I'm agreeing to doing it. I want to know what you think."

When the kids started to whine, Kendra knew what they wanted.

"Milk?" Callum asked.

She nodded and searched her bag for the bottles she had been waiting for them to want. They were so excited to be on the move outside of the condo that neither realized it was past the time for their afternoon bottle.

Callum stood and placed them back in their stroller, lowering the backs just in time for Kendra to silence their cries by handing them their bottles. After she covered them with thin blankets, she moved the stroller closer to her. Callum sat next to her on the sofa. He pulled her close into his embrace.

"What do you think?" she asked.

"I have no problem of an image of me as a father and man who loves his woman out in the public. I would need to see the contract and the exclusivity clause that I know they'll want us to sign. Are you going to have your attorney look over the specifics? I can have one of my company attorneys look over it. We have a new firm out of New York who has been doing amazing work," he offered.

"Adrian Jarreau?"

"Yes. You know of him?"

"There has been a lot of talk about that firm over the past few years. I saw where they made the headlines when they signed you and your brothers on as clients. If you don't mind, can I have everything sent to them for review? I'm not saying yes. I was more concerned about whether or not you wanted to do it. I know you love the boys. I wasn't sure if you wanted that family image of the four of us; together."

"Why wouldn't I want that? I wouldn't deny my love for my sons or for you. I love everything about where my life is right now. My undeniable thirst for you created two beautiful sons. Who I am now isn't who I thought I would be, but I promise you, if given to option to do this again or not, I would choose the three of you every single time. I don't like people making up their own stories about what we are to each other just to get likes, shares or to make money on social media sites. If there is a story, it should come from us as a family. Do you not want that?"

His questioning her seemed like it took his smile away. She must have hit a nerve.

"I don't have a problem with it. I didn't know if you wanted people to get an image of you that wasn't your usual single bachelor thing. I know how men can be."

"Oh? Do you? I don't know what you're trying to say. Can you just say it and stop holding back. What are you saying?"

Kendra exhaled and looked at the boys before responding.

"Okay, here it is. We have been playing house for a while now."

Before she could continue, Callum stretched his arm around her and closed his office door.

"I'm listening," he said.

"What we have has pretty much been a secret, not that people don't know that we have kids together. We haven't exactly been out in the public eye together. We agreed to no social media photos of the boys; at least not yet. I know we're still trying to navigate what we are to each other. A picture like that may not do well with certain audiences."

Callum moved his arm from around her and she was immediately deflated. She'd said the wrong word. His face and body language were a clear indicator.

"Women. You're talking about women. Is that what you think I'm worried about; ever? Let me see if I can read you right. You feel like I've been keeping you and our sons behind a, sort of firewall, away from the public, or women, seeing that I'm with someone as if any of them may have a chance with me? You're not worried about their chance with me. You're worried about what my plans are with them; with any of them. Is that what you think is going on here? You think I'm biding my time, for some reason, with you, with intentions of someone else around the corner? Kendra, what do I have to do so that you believe I'm not interested in someone else? You think my playboy image will be tarnished if I'm seen in a photo with you and our children? Do you even know me? I haven't been hiding you or them? I love all three of you. I thought I was protecting you. How are we not seeing this the same way?"

"Callum, I'm not trying to have a fight with you. I'm treading lightly without knowing where you stand."

"Where I stand? You mean, where you stand. I've been crystal clear about what I want. You. I want you. That hasn't changed since I asked you to give me another chance. Did you think that the chance I was speaking of was a sexual one? I love that with you but that's not all I want with you. The problem is, you can't trust me, can you? I see it in your eyes sometimes, especially if my phone rings or pings with a text message that I don't return. I see the questions in your eyes even when you think I'm not paying attention. You give me all of you every night, but not when we're just living our lives. You think I wouldn't want a beautiful photo opportunity with you and my kids? You think that little of me and my intentions?"

She felt bad. In the back of her mind, she was agreeing with his assessment. She hadn't fully let go of her issues of trust when it came to him. Yes, in Hawaii, he was all about her. What happens when they go back to their lives; hers in Vegas and his all over the country? What about his next trip to visit his friends in Chicago or Las Vegas? She'd seen pictures on social media of him over the past year at that same casino a few times. Maybe she was the problem and not him.

She looked to his office door and wondered if anyone could hear them. She refocused when Finn threw his bottle to the floor and looked over at it. That was his usual signal that he was done. Callum was trying to break him out of that bad habit.

"That's not nice, Finn. No throwing," he said. "Mommy and daddy don't like that. You be nice and hand your bottle and not throw it," Callum added.

They both couldn't help but swoon when Finn giggled and reached for it. She picked it up, wiped off the bottle nipple and handed it back to him.

"No more throwing," she said, confirming Callum's stance.

Putting the bottle back in his mouth, Finn leaned back, his eyes almost immediately closing.

"He is something else," Kendra said.

"And you think I don't live for all of this?"

"We never finished our talk. I guess I'm still a little unsure of us."

"We haven't finished because you wanted to stop. It was getting to be too much for you. Anytime you want to continue that talk, let me know. I am happy to pass the contract information to Adrian to look at. If he's good with what he reads or has changes, and you and I are good with it, I'm very much open to the idea. I am not hiding you and my children. I would go anywhere and show you off to anymore, claiming you as the love of my life. I'm not sure you're ready for that. Why don't we talk when I get in tonight? I shouldn't be later than eight or nine."

There was a knock on Callum's door before she had a chance to respond.

"Yes?" he called out.

The door opened and Leslie poked her head in.

"Hi, Kendra. It's nice to see you again."

Kendra remembered meeting her at the Detroit office before.

"It's good to see you as well."

"Congratulations on the twins. They are absolutely adorable. Callum, your next meeting is in five minutes. The team is gathering in conference room B," Leslie said.

"Thanks."

"I'll bring the boys around for everyone to see before I leave," Kendra said.

"Oh, goody. I'll let everyone know," Leslie said and left the alone, closing the door back.

Callum stood and kissed both boys and then leaned over and kissed her lips. Even though her approach to the conversation had upset him, he still wanted her to know that he loved her.

"I need to get to that meeting. What else are you planning besides the park?" he asked.

"Not a lot. I just wanted to get me and them some fresh air for a bit. Your cousin, Lola, called and asked if I wanted to bring the boys over for a family visit. I will probably do that for a few hours or so. By then, these two will be ready to go home for a little playtime with me before getting them ready for bed. I think the three of us will be down for the count."

"Okay. Have fun and I'll see you tonight. Tellum and Byrum are coming into town in a few days. How about I take tomorrow off and we do some family sightseeing? We can take some of our own pictures while we're out. We'll definitely get some ice cream. I think our boys are hooked on it now."

"That's all your fault. You gave them their first taste of ice cream and now as soon as they see those little vanilla cups, they do a happy dance in their high-chairs."

"Ice cream it is. Up for that kind of day?"

Kendra smiled. She didn't want him to feel any pressure. She simply needed to be sure of her next move with him. A day out would be nice.

"I'd like that. I would love to see more of the Hawaii you spent your childhood summers loving."

"I got you."

Callum kissed her one last time and quickly kissed the boys again and then he hustled out to his meeting. She turned her head to see Leslie trying to follow him with her hurried short steps to his long strides. She loved him, but they still had a lot to talk about.

**

Callum tried to enter their bedroom quietly after getting in a little later than he had planned. When he stepped off of the elevator, he used his phone to unlock the door to the condo and looked at the time. It was a little after ten. Several of his meetings had run over, especially his call with Adrian about the exclusive photoshoot and story about them that Kendra brought to him. Even though that part of the conversation had been quick when they decided to table it until after Adrian had a chance to read it, they talked about new accounts and trusts he wanted set up for the boys and for Kendra. He didn't know where things were headed. He had to settle for what may be his reality. It's possible that Kendra would never let him fully back into her life. They were heading toward two years since they had broken up. That was still a few months away. They were closer physically, but Kendra was still keeping a part of herself from him. He wasn't sure he'd ever get that back.

When he opened the bedroom door where it was ajar, his eyes caught sight of Kendra's perfectly sculpted body in bed. He smiled because she wasn't just in it, she was on the side that he usually slept on. Her body was curved around his pillow. His heart was so full of love and adoration for all that she was; for all that she'd given up for their sons. If only he could get her to trust him with her heart again, he would never do anything that would make her question her decision to let him in. He wanted to hold her forever. He wanted to love her for an eternity. He wanted all of her.

Stepping back out of the room, he went into the other bedroom to get his nightly kiss. He looked at their heart monitors which were also linked not just to the hospital but also to his phone and Kendra's phone. Things were looking up. He looked at his phone several times a day to check on them. He only hoped that the love he had for all of them would be enough to hold them together as one.

"Okay, my boys. I need you to work on your mom from your end and I'll do the same from mine."

Kissing them one last time, he walked back into the bedroom where Kendra lay unmoved. He tiptoed into the bathroom to get a shower, hopefully without waking her.

He stepped under the running hot water and stood with his hands braced against the wall. His mind and his heart were heaving in thought. He was ready for the next level with Kendra. While she was preoccupied with the idea that she may not be enough for him, he struggled with if he were doing enough to show her that he wanted the world to know that he loved and wanted her. He loved his little family. The idea of them was unexpected but welcomed more than anything else he had in his life. He would give it all up just to have them. He thought about things he'd seen on social media about what people would do different in life. He remembered a story of a woman who said that she didn't enjoy motherhood. She had two kids with a man who wasn't worth the ground he walked on, according to the stories he'd also read about the man. They were a high-profile couple, so their story wasn't a secret. When asked if she would do anything different, she offered that she would go back and not have kids; not anyone's kids. She realized motherhood wasn't for her. Still, she was doing the best with what she had.

Callum thought about that question. If he could go back, what he would change is the night with Tessa. He would still want Kendra and definitely still want his sons. He wouldn't trade that part of this life for anything. Of everything that he has amassed, nothing even came close to the love he has for Kendra and the boys.

Making quick work of his shower, he turned off the water before stepping out and quickly toweled dry. He would clean up the bathroom in the morning before they headed out for their family day. Right now, he needed his woman. He needed her to know how much he wanted and would always want her.

Walking back into the bedroom, he pulled back the covers and slipped in naked behind Kendra. He looked underneath and found her in one of his t-shirts. When his hands roamed over her behind, he found a very thin stringed thong.

Sliding his body down, he kissed his way down her back to her behind. Palming both cheeks, he kissed from one side to the other, going back and forth, slowly and methodically. He moaned out his happiness when Kendra's hand reached down and caressed his head, not pushing him away but encouraging him on.

"You're home," she said softly.

"I am and I missed you. I'm sorry about earlier. I was a little cold with you. I didn't mean to be."

Kissing his way back up her body, he found her shoulder and then her neck, making sure his lips connected with every part of her.

"I know you didn't. I'm sorry. I love you. I do love you. The issues I have are me. I need to deal with that. Don't think that this has anything to do with doubting you."

Callum kissed her earlobe and spoke right into her ear.

"I know what this has to deal with. Whatever time you need to work through allowing me back in fully, I'm going to be here until you do."

Callum slipped her panties from her body and moved in close behind her. He inhaled her sweet, lavender scent. Instantaneously, his body began to sing a romantic tune that had him forgetting about his busy day in order to focus on loving her. The feel of her nakedness against his was always a turn-on. His body responded in-kind to knowing that his body was ready for hers and always would be. He only needed to see her to want her. Smelling her beauty, he desired her. Being inside of her, he would always have a thirst for her. When he lowered his hand to the area between her legs, she was ready for him.

"I was dreaming about you," Kendra softly said.

"Whew, baby. I can feel just how fantastic that dream must have been."

When her behind pushed back slowly, and grinded into him, he replaced his hand with his penis, thick, swollen and prepared to drive them wild. He entered her to them equally groaning. They moved together as one, slowly, enjoying every part of each other.

"I feel you," Kendra whispered to him over her shoulder.

"I can do this with you for the rest of my life and never get enough,"

Callum's voice was strained. He was doing his hardest to draw out their pleasure. From behind, Kendra was tight and enclosed around him like she never wanted to let him go. That's what he was hoping for.

Raising their right hands above their heads and placing them locked together on the pillow, he raised a leg and stroked her deeper He was intent on building a fire with nothing available in the world to douse it.

She gasped.

He moaned.

Kendra threw her behind back at him and he surged sharply, in and out and then around. His passion grew as his need rose as he strained to hold on longer. He worked hard to breathe through gritted teeth.

Minutes later, he quickened the pace and felt her body tremor with a pulsating release. He followed her into ecstasy as he released his essence into the depths of her womanhood. He was so deeply seated into her that there was no doubt that they were one.

On one last thrust into her body, he released a heavy sigh of relief against her skin. Lowering their arms and with her in his tight embrace, they slipped into slumber.

# 10

Native Hawaiian folk music flowed across the air. Kendra moved her hips to the sound of one of Hawaii's top artists who was supported by a live band in the background. His melodies were smooth and prevented anyone from sitting still. She couldn't remember his name that Leilani had shared with her. Whoever it was, she made a mental note to look him up at a later date.

"Are you having a great time?" Leilani asked her.

"I am. Thanks for inviting me out. Usually, Callum and I aren't out of the house at the same time. This is the last night his brothers are in town and he wanted to hang out with them. I don't think they get to do that too often unless it's about work. When our nanny, who is also a nurse, said that she was available to watch the boys tonight, he practically pushed me out of the front door to come out to dinner with you and your friends tonight," Kendra explained.

"I'm going to need the information on where you got this white lace halter top. I love it. I don't have the perfect shape like you do, but who cares these days. If women can go out in those bubble skirts without second guessing it, I can wear a halter top and throw these large puppies up in them," Leilani said as they continued to sway to the beat.

The group was enjoying a night out at a luau that included male and female fire dancers, a large variety of island exclusive cuisine that Kendra delighted in. While others had fruity drinks with alcohol, she took her alcohol-free. They were just as delicious. She was enjoying live music and the most spectacular fire knife tricks that she'd ever seen.

A few days ago, Callum had taken her out to dinner and then to a local beach where they checked out a fire knife event from the sand. She was happy that she got to experience one this up close and personal. They were dancing right in front of her.

The other two ladies, close friends of Leilani's danced their way back over to the table. When two men walked up and asked her and Leilani to dance, she said sure. After a while, Leilani danced with both men. Kendra returned to the table and sat down. When their waiter walked over, she ordered a bottle of water.

"You haven't had a grownup drink since we've been out," the woman named Shar leaned over and spoke above the music.

"What gives?" Paris asked, another friend of Leilani's who was visiting from Miami, Florida.

"I still pump for my twins. No alcohol for me until after they are a year old. They're getting close to that but not close enough," Kendra shared.

"That's right, you have twins with Callum Blackstone. You're gorgeous. I see why he's all over you and populating. If Callum is known for anything, it's beautiful women. Are you living here with him? Leilani mentioned her cousin had twins who had some health issues but are better now. Those your twins?" Paris asked.

"Yes. Thankfully, they are getting healthier by the day."

"Does that mean you'll be going back home soon? I mean, I'm not trying to rush you away or anything. I'm just saying that usually when I'm in town and I run into Callum, he's out partying hard with us. He would be all up in a place like this. Women would hear that he was here and they would come out in droves just to try and catch his eye. With you here, you must have him under lock and key," Shar said.

Both women giggled to each other before they turned back in her direction.

"He's not under lock and key. Callum is free to do whatever he wants. I know work is important and that keeps him busy. He's also an amazing father. He spends a lot of time bonding with them."

"Callum Blackstone?" both women questioned together loudly.

When they tumbled back with heavy laughter, Kendra didn't quite grasp where the joke was.

"What do you mean?" she curiously asked.

"No one in the world would have ever pictured Callum Blackstone as baby making material. I mean, that brother has to have stock in condom companies. He's well known on this island. I guess you don't know much about his life when you're not here. I don't remember seeing you over the past year that he's been here. Where have you been before now?" Shar asked.

Kendra's shoulders slumped. She looked to the dance floor where Leilani waved at her as she danced between two different men. She couldn't look to her to get rescued. She faced the inquisitive women. Without Leilani at the table, it was clear the women didn't care for her presence.

"I live in Las Vegas."

"Ah, that makes sense. Callum has been back and forth to Hawaii a lot over the past year. I don't remember him ever saying that he had a kid on the way, let alone two of them. It's hard to believe he was caught slipping. Word is he is quite serious about not making any babies. I guess his little swimmers found a way with you. That's sad news for the women of the world," Paris declared.

"I think it's extra sad for the women here in Hawaii. I once tried to turn his eye my way. I was biding my time knowing that he was all about business for some time now. Imagine my surprise when I asked about him when I arrived and Leilani mentioned you. I thought the two of you were just an item for social media. I didn't know it was that serious. Do you still play ball? I'm assuming you have to get back home for that," Shar asked.

Kendra was losing patience. She didn't know if the women were purposely trying to be disrespectful, trying to get a rise out of her or trying to make her think that Callum was someone else when not around her. She was both curious and annoyed by their incessant questioning. She took a sip from the water bottle that the waiter placed in front of her. Before answering, she also, nonchalantly popped a large grilled shrimp in her mouth.

"I don't play anymore. I'm not sure I will. With twins, my life is busy around the clock."

"Because I'm sure Callum is still Callum, all about himself. What, he didn't get you a houseful of nannies to help you? Don't tell me he's changing diapers and doing feedings through the night. That is not the Callum we know. He's usually a little more preoccupied with women a lot older than twin babies. Perhaps, he's holding back until he's here alone again. I know the women are waiting for that. I hear they've been checking the tight security around the resort for when he's there. Too bad no one is allowed on the property. I had actually thought about getting a job there. Lots of sexy men around that place, with him leading the pack. All of that...sorry, I don't mean to be disrespectful. I'm not used to having to hold back my words when it comes to him. He's so fine," Shar said.

"That he is. Are you two still together or just being parents?"

Kendra got it. They are trying to get an emotional rise out of her by insinuating that Callum's playboy ways are only stifled because she and the boys were in Hawaii. She didn't know how to answer the question. She uttered her best response until she could focus her thoughts without the images they were trying to put in her head.

"We're figuring things out. Right now, our focus is on making sure our sons' health problems are no longer a major problem."

"Where is he tonight? You're here alone while he's someplace else alone? I think Leilani said you were able to get out tonight because you got a sitter. That means it's not him."

"He's out with his brothers having dinner and playing pool."

Shar sat up straight.

"Wait – you mean to tell me, I'm here with all of you women tonight and there are three very fine, very sexy Blackstone men in town? Hell, do you know what pool hall they went to? There are several that are popular. We're at the wrong party," Shar exclaimed.

Kendra sipped on her water some more.

"Any of them will do, well, not Callum, of course because he's yours right, or is he?"

Kendra shrugged off their attempts to push her buttons.

"As I said before, Callum is free to do as he pleases," she said.

Kendra's temperature was rising. She was about to lose her cool with their prodding and assumptions.

"Damn, y'all open with it and stuff? I tried that open thing with my ex-boyfriend, Akamu, but he started seeing too many women when we only agreed to be open to one woman on the side for him and one man on the side for me," Shar admitted.

Kendra's mind said that Shar was oversharing too much personal information. They were not saying the same thing. No way in hell would she ever decide to be involved with a man who needed a chick on the side. Is that what Tessa was for him when he cheated with her? Questions rose up and plagued her psyche.

"I don't roll like that," Kendra replied.

"Oh, so are you letting him just get it out of his system while y'all are figuring it out?"

"Figuring what out?" Leilani asked rejoining them around the table.

Kendra handed Leilani her glass that she'd left on the table.

"Oh, nothing," Paris said with eyes flying from Leilani to Kendra. Shar and Paris faked like they had no idea what the conversation was about as they sipped longer on their drinks than they had been doing. Kendra guessed the question was for her. She turned to Leilani. She wanted some truth.

"They were telling me about the part of Callum that I don't know about; his life here in Hawaii before I showed up; his knack for going through condoms like they you go through candy bars and other sordid ideas that they seem to want me to believe. Am I missing and messing something up when it comes to him?" she asked Leilani.

Kendra didn't know if Callum's cousin would protect him or speak the truth, if the ideal was two different things. Instead of answering, Leilani turned her eyes to her two friends. Her smile gone. It was now replaced by a grim look of embarrassment.

"What the hell are the two of you filling her head with about him? You both speak from a place of lust for him. You have each had eyes for him. What? Are you feeling out Kendra to see if you can talk her out of his life? Kill that *right* now! I'm sorry,

Kendra. These two are probably drunk. They mean no harm. You know Callum loves you," she said.

"Love? Callum Blackstone in love?" Shar shouted and then laughed so hard that she knocked her drink from the ground-level table.

"Maybe you should go get yourself another drink and take Paris with you," Leilani suggested.

Kendra watched her shoo her two friends away from the table.

"That was interesting," Kendra mumbled.

"I'm so sorry for my friends. They can be rather up front, too personal and quite crass. Callum never had an interest in either of them. In fact, I think Shar has made a play for Tellum, Byrum and Callum at one time or another. She grew up here. They spent every summer here through their late teens until they started spending their summers on their college campuses. Ignore those catty women. I love them like sisters but they can be a lot at times."

"It's okay. It's getting late anyway. I want the sitter to be able to get home at a decent hour. I'm going to get back to the condo. Thanks for inviting me out. I really did have a good time. I'll stop by the house and bring the boys by soon?" she said standing.

"That would be great. You drove here, right? Do you need me to walk you out?"

"Oh, no. I'm parked right near the front entrance. The valets will watch for me, I'm sure. Thanks again for a fun night out. I needed this."

Before Leilani could say anything else, Kendra straightened her skirt and headed for the door.

"Bye, Kendra. Tell Callum we said hello!" she heard Shar yell as she walked near the bar, but not right next to it.

She could hear them giggling as she kept going without stopping or acknowledging them. She despised women who deliberately got under your skin just to get a reaction. They practically tried to tell her that Callum was a bed hopper and would still be if she wasn't around.

Exiting the bar, she pressed the alert button on the remote to light up the truck with the internal lights and the outside running lights. With hard, purposeful steps, she practically ran to the truck with a mound of questions and doubt in her mind.

Pulling into traffic, she thought about what they said about what Callum would be getting into if she wasn't around. Jealously, she knew was a dangerous thing. She was prone to that more now than before he cheated on her.

She tried to focus on the life that they had been living the past few months. She wondered if it was real. Seeing him with Tessa played over and over again in her head. She couldn't turn the image off as her anxiety rose to an unhealthy level. That, and what those women said had her making a left turn at the next light instead of going straight on the main road which was fifteen minutes from home. She pulled over to the side of the busy road and pulled out her phone. Googling the name of the place that Callum mentioned he was going to, she found out that it was only ten minutes away from where she was. Before she put the truck back in drive, she waited and thought about what she was about to do. It was situations like this in movies and on social media that led women to find out what they didn't really want to know about. She was here now.

Her mind was all over the place. She couldn't turn around and go home now. Every part of her was securely invested in what Callum was doing. This is where cheating was taking her. This is where jealousy was leading her. This is what happens when women let other women get in their heads. No longer second-guessing herself enough to just let it go and go home, Kendra put the truck in drive and followed where Google Maps was taking her. She had to know.

It didn't take her long to get to the pool hall. As soon as she pulled up, someone was pulling out of a parking space at the door. That was another sign that she made the right choice. In her head as she drove, she promised that if she couldn't find a parking space, she would go home. She pulled right up and a space became available.

She looked to her left and there was the car that Tellum had rented. She remembered seeing it over the past few days. Tellum was driving them tonight. There was another sign – she immediately spotted the car which let her know that they were still here.

Parking, she got out and walked on nervous, shaky legs to the door. Once inside, there was no cover charge, so the man at the door allowed her to pass by him. She walked down a long hall where music blared so loud that she felt like the walls around her were shaking. They were definitely sweating.

Passing through throngs of people, she walked into a wide-open area that had over twenty pool tables scattered across the large room. There were also tables full of people eating and drinking. In the center of the room was a large dance floor that was also crowded. Her eyes then landed on Tellum and Byrum, who were around a pool table laughing with a group of men. Callum was not with them. Not going in that direction, she walked around, placing her hands inside of the pockets of her skirt. Her head turned and gazed at everyone as she went in search of Callum. She was about to turn around and go back the way she came when a sight caught her eye. Down a slim hallway, she saw a woman leaning against the wall. She had on a very tight little white dress. Standing in front of her and leaning forward, too close for her comfort, was Callum. She couldn't move. The moment looked private. It looked intimate. She was seeing this before her eyes; again. The only thing different this time was that she didn't walk into a hotel room to find this woman riding him. If she stayed long enough, that may be what will end up happening.

As fast as her legs could carry her, she turned and raced back toward the entrance, tears flowing down her face.

"Miss? Are you alright?"

Kendra heard the man at the door calling after her. She couldn't stop. All she wanted to do was get home. Not just get home to the condo, but get home to Las Vegas. She had to be done with Callum once and for all. No more of his lies. He was never going to change. He only offered her that because he got caught. She was done.

Getting into the truck, she threw it into drive and sped off. She wiped the falling tears from her eyes to make sure she could see as she drove home.

"I'm not only done with you, Callum Blackstone. I am *DONE, DONE!*" she shouted into the night air.

# 11

Callum put Finn and Liam in their car seats while trying to keep his eyes on Kendra. Her reactions to him since last night have left him confused. The evening before, when he left her still getting dressed to go out with his cousin, she was her normal, usual, happy self. She was excited to be going out to have a girls' night out. She hadn't done that since she left Vegas where he knew she had several close friends she would hang out with and travel with; some on the team and others she'd known for years before she joined her home team.

Even after leaving the appointment with Dr. Myers who flew in to give the boys a thorough checkup where he told them that he didn't believe the heart monitors were needed any longer, he didn't get the joy and level of excitement he thought he would get from her. Not once did she look his way. Her smiles were fake; just as fake as her responses to him.

When he came home from the pool hall the night before, after checking on the boys, he joined her in bed after a shower to wash off the smell of smoke and alcohol. When he pulled her close to him, the way they often slept, she pushed him away and said, not tonight. That was a first for her. Kendra loved sleeping in his arms. If he wasn't so tired, since it was after midnight, he would have turned on a light and talked through what was on her mind. He couldn't imagine what had happened, considering they had spent the evening apart.

When he woke up, Kendra was already up getting the kids dressed for their appointment. He left the bedroom and walked into the family room where she was putting bibs around their necks. He remembered her saying that the slobbering from teething, as more were coming in, had gotten worse. Now when she took them out, she always put outfit-matching bibs on them. He tried talking to her and all he got was one-word answers. When he asked her why she didn't wake him so that he could help get them ready, she simply said, she had it. He asked her if she needed his help getting their bag together, she said, she could do it herself. The coldness of her responses were strange for her. The last time she was this cold to him was... He didn't even want to think about that night. He thought that was behind them. Was she back in that moment? Was she reliving that night once again? They hadn't spent any more time talking about that time because things were going so well.

Something had changed. He didn't want to poke the bear. He was already nervous about this doctor appointment. This was the one where they would find out if the surgery had worked as expected.

The appointment was perfect. The boys were perfect. He thought that he and Kendra were too.

"Dr. Myers made our day, didn't he?" he asked, climbing in the back to his usual seat between the boys.

He looked her way and again, no emotion. She sat with her eyes facing forward and both hands on the steering wheel. She wasn't even turning around to smile or giggle at the boys even though they were in a playful mood talking and laughing in each other's direction. That was something new they were doing. They finally figured out that where one of them went, the other went. They had their own conversation going on. He continued to try to engage Kendra as she pulled out into traffic.

He asked her about the night before and whether she had a good time. Her response, yes. That was it. He asked her what time did she get in. Her response, she didn't remember. He tried asking if the boys were wide awake when she got home. Her answer, no. Callum finally decided to let the moment go. Whatever was on her mind, she didn't want to talk about it. If he had done something, he wished that she would tell him; talk to him about it. Talk to him about anything at this point. He wanted his jovial baby back. She had been in such a happy space with him that whatever was wrong, had to be big.

They drove in silence back to the condo. He was excited because he'd had a plan that both of his brothers had been in on. The last thing he wanted to do was engage her in any way that would ruin how great the day could actually turn out to be.

They arrived at the condo. Without any words being spoken between them, Kendra hustled out of the truck and went to open the back to take out the stroller. Callum kept his eyes on her though it appeared the last place she wanted her eyes to land was on him. He had to stay focused on the plan for the night.

Before today, they had already decided that they would stay home and delight in any good news they had received. He couldn't wait to tell their families. He knew his mother was waiting by the phone to hear from him.

Once he had them loaded in the stroller, before he could close the door to the truck and grab their baby bag from the floor of the truck, Kendra had already walked ahead of him. To his dismay, not only did she do that, but she got in the elevator and let the door close before he could join them. Something was really bad; not just semi-bad, but seriously bad. Taking his time, Callum tried to play the events of the night before and this morning in his head to see what he had missed. If he were a mind reader, as his father would often say about their mother, he would already know what direction to move in. Her silent treatment was the worse. He couldn't respond to that.

When he finally arrived, Kendra was already undressing the boys in their room. She'd put out blue onesies to put them in.

"Do you need help?" he asked her, placing the bag in the rocking chair in the corner of the room.

"No," she curtly replied. He, once again, let it go and turned and left the room. He could hear the boys calling for him as he walked out. Not making them be punished because she was punishing their father for some unknown reason, he walked back over to their changing table where Liam was kicking and rolling over to avoid getting his clothes changed. He reached down and picked up Finn, who Kendra had placed in the crib. He moved to stand beside her to let Liam know that he was near when she stopped moving. He watched her head drop before she turned to him.

"What is wrong?" he asked.

"You do it. I'm going to lay down."

Without any explanation for her mood, he did just that. He picked Liam up and placed them both in the crib. He wasn't as good at multitasking as Kendra was. He needed them together to keep his eyes on them. They were moving more and crawling everywhere. He would often be out of breath chasing behind them. There was no doubt that they were feeling much better.

He playfully talked with them and tickled them until he had them changed. Rubbing their bellies, he picked up their baby bag, and pulled out two bottles. Both avidly reached for theirs and quieted down. He needed a few moments with Kendra. He turned on the camera over their crib and went out into the living room. He hoped that what he had planned for her, which he was going to do later, but decided to do now, would brighten her day. He promised her that he would show and prove. He was about to do that.

Reaching into the closet, he found what he'd hidden in his backpack the night before. He took a huge breath and after looking in on the kids one last time, he walked into the bedroom where he found Kendra laying across the bed with her back to him. Her usual routine of laying in the family room until the boys were asleep had changed. This time, laying down meant on the bed.

He wanted to talk, but maybe in a few moments, she would be in a better mindset to do so.

Reaching for the remote to the music sound bar, he clicked until he found the song he needed for this moment. When the song started, he knelt in position and prayed she would turn around and see him at his most vulnerable state.

Callum got his wish. She knew the song. She heard the lyrics start. It was their song by Marvin Gaye and Tammi Terrell.

"*Like sweet morning dew*," Callum sang.

Kendra shot up off the bed and stared at him. There was no sign of love, affection or tolerance. He saw anger and frustration. His arm was extended with a small black velvet ring box opened to the ring that he'd had custom made for her over a week ago. Byrum had the task of making sure it got to Hawaii with him when he arrived.

His hopes were immediately dashed. She looked at the ring and then back at him. He stopped singing. He reached for the remote to the soundbar with his free hand. Silenced lived between them. It was now or never, despite the hurtful look on her face. He was hoping for a lot more joy.

"No, Callum."

He let out a huge breath and then stood. He'd had enough of guessing.

"Okay, what the hell did I do? You've been walking around her like I committed a crime or something since last night. You left here to go out and came home an entirely different person than the one I left here getting dressed. What could I have done in that short period of time? What?" he begged.

He looked at her. Her hands were balled into fists at her side. Her face looked like she wished she had something to throw at him. Kendra was looking at him as if she were disgusted by him. He waited. They had to talk this out.

"I'm going home. I'm going back to Las Vegas. The boys and I are leaving tomorrow."

That was it. That's all she said. He was left shocked to his very core. She was leaving? Just like that? She was taking his sons with her?

"Whoa, wait a minute," he said following her into the walk-in closet.

His eyes stayed on her as she grabbed the two large suit cases she kept there. She placed one up on the bed and opened it. She didn't move to put anything in it yet. He tried reaching for it and she moved it out of his grasp.

"I'm going home, Callum. You won't be able to talk me out of it. My mother booked a flight for me and the kids. I think I've spent enough time here. The doctor gave them the all clear today. They can fly and do normal things. I need to get back to my life."

Callum closed the ring box and put it in his pants pocket.

"Just like that? All you have to say is you're leaving and you're taking my kids almost three thousand miles away? What is wrong? Talk to me? Did something happen? You're shutting me down and giving me the cold silent treatment again. I won't get to see them if you take them away. Why would you do this?"

"You can come see them anytime you want. I would never keep them away from you."

"But you would take them away. Can you imagine what that would do to them? To me? To us?"

"There is no us, Callum. I don't know why I thought there ever could be."

"You didn't come here for me to be a part-time father or part-time lover. That's what you're turning me into if you leave like this."

"You'll never be a part-time father. They love you. We will figure this out."

"And us?"

"I just said that there is no us. You can get back to your life of being the free and fancy playboy, ladies' man, ultimate bachelor or whatever the lingo is these days. I have to make a life for me too."

"The photo shoot. We're not doing that now?"

"We're not really that kind of family. Were we ever going to be, I doubt it. This has been a fantasy being here. It really isn't what reality is about. I just want to go home, Callum."

Callum dropped his shoulders in defeat. He knew *this* Kendra. She wasn't going to change her mind. When she is set on leaving him, she does it. He remembered her leaving him before and never even trying to reach out to him. He couldn't have that again. She had his children.

"What's changed. Two nights ago, we were making love. Last night I tried to love on you and you pushed me away like I was vermin. You came here for my help and what, you got that and now you want to roll out? Is this payback for what I did?

You come here, introduce me to my sons, had me love them, had me loving all on you and then you just snatch them away?"

"I'm done, Callum. Can we just leave it at that? I want to go home. I'm sorry I'm taking the boys. You have the means and your own jet to fly anywhere you want, when you want. Our door is always open to you in Vegas. Never would I deny you access to them."

"But you're taking away all access to you?"

"All of it."

Before he could really dive in, one of the boys started crying. When he started to go check on them, she stopped him.

"I got them. I have to get used to caring for them by myself unless you come see them."

"Are you serious, right now? We're done? We're over? No explanation? No story? No, kiss my ass, Callum, you're trash for what you did to me and this is your payback? You don't have anything to say at all other than you're leaving."

Kendra stopped at the doorway and turned to him.

"Yes. My flight is at eight in the morning tomorrow. I'll sleep on the rollaway bed in the room with the boys tonight. If you'd like to take us to the airport, I would appreciate it. If not, make sure you're up early to say goodbye before I call a car service."

Kendra slammed the bedroom door in his face. Callum was left standing with his face in his hands. His world had just crashed and burned without any warning. He was losing his woman. He was losing his sons. He didn't have time to process any of it. He started to follow her to continue talking but something told him that she was all talked out. He should be used to this Kendra by now. He remembered the last time she walked out and left him. She had not looked back in his direction until she had to. With them healthy and her need for him over, she was again walking out of his life.

Callum turned and sat down on the bed, taking the box out of his pocket. This is not where he thought his life would be. Was this his karma? If so, he didn't like it one bit.

He lowered his head in his hands and then threw the box across the room. Every part of him was shattered. Still, at the end of it all, he still found himself loving her, wanting her, thirsting for her. How could she change so fast?

"What the hell happened?" he said out loud to himself.

Kendra was leaving *Quiet Whisper* and taking his heart with her. He was defeated.

# 12

Callum relaxed in the backseat of Mercedes wagon as his driver sped from the Las Vegas airport to get him to Kendra's place in record time. As it was, his time with his sons will be cut short because he and Tellum had a very important meeting in Detroit that he had to get back to. He had already spent more than a week in Detroit taking care of business. He cleared his schedule for two days so that Finn and Liam could set eyes on him before he headed back to Detroit. In two days, he had to get to Hawaii. All of the festivities leading up to Byrum and Keiko's wedding were going to be in full effect.  He was already pretty much operating on fumes these days.

"Callum Blackstone," he said, answering his phone the minute it rang.

"Hey, man. It's Lucas. Where are you? I stopped by your office in Detroit to thank you for letting me use your jet last week to get to New York for a meeting."

"Hey, nothing but the best for one of my best friends. I hope your meeting was a success."

Callum yawned again, this time louder than he thought it would be.

"Was that a yawn? You've been doing that a lot lately. You're not someplace getting some sleep? You went from New York, to Detroit where you told me you had days and nights full of meetings and huddles. I assumed I'd catch you at least heading towards some down time."

"Yes and no. I just landed in Vegas. I'm going to spend some time with my sons before the next week which will be crazy with wedding stuff for Byrum."

"Right. Thanks for getting me the invite to the wedding. It's the talk on all social media sites of how another successful, handsome Black man is off the market. He's got himself a real one, that's for sure."

"Yeah, they are pretty perfect for each other. I'm happy for him."

"I thought I was going to hear wedding bells in the near future for you. What's going on with you and Kendra? I didn't miss that you just said you were on your way to visit your sons but you didn't mention Kendra."

"That's over. I can't do this with her anymore. I haven't told anyone but as you know, she left Hawaii and moved back to Las Vegas, taking my sons with her. It's her right to do whatever she wants with her life. I was hoping they would stay in Hawaii a little longer with me. Truth is, I asked her to marry me and she turned me down. That led to a large blowout a few days later over what we actually mean to each other. Out of that, she decided that what we had wasn't worth fighting for. I don't know what she wants anymore. What I do know is that I'm no longer going to be a willing participant in her play of trying to tear me down for what I did. I have to realize this is how life is going to be. I don't care if my sons are out of the country, I will fly, walk, swim and crawl to spend time with them. That is something I won't allow her to take from me. She can deny me her, but not my sons. Hence, I took yet another flight to see them because I know I'll be busy. As soon as the wedding is over, I'm going to pick the boys up and take them with me to Detroit for a few weeks. They are about to turn a year old. She did agree to having their first birthday party in Detroit. That is, at least, one win for me. I'm going to fly out of Hawaii right after the ceremony is over. I'll head back here to Vegas, pick them up and then we're out. She'll meet us there a week later for the party that my mom is putting together. I'm really starting to hate flying. I never thought I'd be in the air this much now that the resort is pretty much completed."

"She's not going to the wedding? I thought she was invited."

"She was. She told me she thought it best to not go so that people didn't get the wrong impression about her and I. By people, she means me, for starters. I'm over the fight. It's tiring. After all of these months of breaking my back to prove to her who I can be for her and my boys, she flat out told me no, she didn't want to marry me. So, I'm here to focus on them. I'm going to give her the space from me that she wants."

"Man, these women have no idea what they want from us. I've been where you are. Angel and I are still going back and forth to court over my son and how much money she wants. It changes depending on how angry she is with me. I will drag her before I let her get full custody of my son without a fight. This is year three of our court battle. I don't know when that will end. If she wants a fight, that's what she'll get. I admire you, bro. What I'm not going to do is fly all over the world to catch up with my son because she wants to be all over the place. She drains me financially, which I'm about to fight as well. Why a woman would need five figures a month to take care of one child, I don't know. You have two. I bet Kendra is breaking the bank on you, huh?"

His comment had Callum sitting up straight to be sure his friend didn't think their situations were the same. He cleared his throat to focus his mind. Lucas hearing and understanding him was important.

"She won't need to break the bank. It's only money. I let her have whatever she wants. I bought her a new house to make it easier for her and the boys. She was in a condo but this is better because there is a yard for my sons to play and run around in. I also got her a new truck because she's got two car seats. Besides, I want them safe and not in her sleek BMW. It's cute, but not to travel with the boys. I gave her a black card to get whatever she needs either for her or for them. Women go through a lot taking care of children. As men, we shouldn't question what it is, especially if we have it. I didn't have children by a woman who would take from me unnecessarily. This isn't about her, it's about them."

"Really? That's crazy and outrageous. These girls out here will go mad shopping crazy with a black card. I make Angel send my attorney a list of what she needs before I send her any money. Right now, she's only getting what is court ordered, not a dime more. She cut me off, especially off with her and she thinks I'm going to finance her life, probably with another man all up in her. Hell no. Not on my dime. You know these chicks aren't spending a lot of the money they get on a kid."

"You and I are not the same, Lucas. I hear you and I understand why you feel the way you do. There are some women out here who are more materialistic than loving. I messed up with Kendra. Her not wanting me is my fault. What I will never do is punish her or my sons for any reason."

"Wait until she hits you with papers for custody and a boatload of money. You think you know her."

"I do know her. What I know for a fact is that she has no reason to even think about doing that. We've never even had to talk about that. We filed the papers to have their last name changed to Blackstone. In fact, I had forgotten about that and she brought it up because she hated that she didn't do it in the beginning. There was no ill-will, even in the beginning. She didn't do it when they were born because she didn't want to assume that since we weren't together, that I would want them to have my last name. She already knows that I don't care what it is she needs, just get it or let me know and I'll make sure she gets it. We may not be a couple but we are parents to two amazing little boys who love both of us. I don't want to fight in court over money and visitation. I can see them whenever I want. She knows that they are already set with trusts. I've even set her up just in case something happens to me. She's not a gold digger. She has a plan for her life. She's more of a goal, G.O.A.L. digger, bro. Our women are not the same. She sets up video chats with them even though they don't have a clue what I'm saying. It means everything to me that despite us not working out, she knows how important they are to me. Our situations are different. I love Kendra even if she can't look at me without seeing what I did with Tessa. You and Angel were never in a relationship. No disrespect, but we are not the same. As a man, your main concern should be your son. I am bone tired. Still, my sons don't know anything about that. They only know when they see me, I'm daddy. So, yes, here I am on my way again to see them because as their father, I want them to know that I will always be here. Look, I just pulled up. I'll hit you at the wedding."

Callum was done explaining to a grown-ass man that life is about the children when you start having them. The best thing to do is make sure that life is peaceful even in a broken situation between the parents.

"Yeah, you will. Thanks for this conversation. I know it wasn't long yet, it was impactful. I hear you. Perhaps, Angel and I need to have a conversation that isn't so fiery."

"You said it and not me."

Callum grabbed the two bags from the seat next to him and made his way to Kendra's front door. He would check into his hotel after getting hugs and kisses from Finn and Liam.

Before he could ring the bell, the door opened and Kendra was on the other side. There was awkward silence before she moved to the side to let him in. He hadn't had much conversation with her unless it was about the kids since that last night in Hawaii. As he entered the house, he noticed she still had a lot to unpack after moving into the new house.

"How are you?" he asked.

"I'm fine. Still unpacking."

"The boys asleep?"

"No. They're in the playroom with my mother. My dad is out back doing some stuff. Go on up. I'm sure they'll be wide awake when they see you."

Callum headed toward the steps and remembered the bags.

"I have some things for the boys."

Handing her the bags, he waited while she opened one of them and smiled.

"Stuffed ambulances. They will love these. They love everything they can find to get their hands on. Thanks for these. I'm glad these are plush. They now throw everything so the plastic ones could be used as weapons. They take great humor in hitting each other with something," she kidded.

Callum smiled even though the space between them was still weird. He pointed to the bags.

"There are a few other things inside. You don't have to thank me. I'm their father. Did you find the new cribs you wanted now that you're splitting them up?"

"I haven't. I know you asked me the last time you were here when we moved in. I haven't forgotten. I may be hesitant about putting them into two cribs. They're so close and used to being next to each other when they wake up. The change may turn out to be more of an issue for me than for them. They are getting too big to sleep in the same crib. They still seem to love it."

"When they are together, as long as they can see each other they're fine. I have noticed that. Anyway, I'm going to go up and spend some time with them. I'll be around until tomorrow evening. I need to get some sleep. Tomorrow, I'm hoping to stay a little longer than today. I'll be at my hotel if you need anything. Otherwise, I'm flying back out late tomorrow evening, around midnight. I have some business in Detroit before heading to *Quiet Whisper*. You're still not going to the wedding?"

Callum knew the answer. There was no doubt that Kendra wanted to go to the wedding. For some reason, she was being stubborn. She, Keiko and Cheyenne had become quite close. Avoiding him by not going to the wedding wasn't logical. It wasn't his job to change her mind. She's made her intentions about them extremely clear. He finally got it. He wouldn't press her to be with him anymore. If he never got a message before, he definitely got one that night when he played their song and it had no impact on her. In fact, it had a negative impact.

"I have a lot to do. I called Keiko to let her know that I wouldn't be attending. I'm still settling in here. Besides, I haven't been away from the boys for more than a day or a..."

When she didn't finish, he knew she meant to say more than a night. She wouldn't say it because that would mean she was remembering the nights she'd spent with him.

Even though they were all there, they stole time away when her mother or the nanny was there to keep an eye on their sons. Those nights were steamy, sexy and as spicy as they could get without limits. What he loved about being with her was how each time was better than the last. Images plagued both of them as they connected without words being said. They were thinking the same thing. Not wanting to revisit anything, he turned and raced up the steps, calling for Finn and Liam as he took the steps two at a time.

He hated leaving Kendra standing in the middle of the room looking like she wanted to say more, but couldn't bring herself to do so. He would no longer pull feelings out of her. If and when she had something to say to him, he would listen. For now, the minute he heard his sons babble, he knew they heard his voice.

As soon as he peaked into the playroom where they were seated on matts on the floor, both cried with arms reaching for him. He did what he usually did to not make either of them wait, he lifted both of them up in his arms. With hands and arms flying with excitement, he rained down kisses and hugs on them.

"Callum, it's always good to see you."

"Oh, I'm so sorry. I just missed them so much. Anytime I see how excited they are to see me, I just want to eat them up. Ms. Melissa, it's always great to see you too. How are things?"

When he attempted to set the boys down so that he could get his suit jacket off, both cried immediately and reached back for him.

"Look at them. They are only like that with you. Not even Kendra gets this kind of greeting."

Callum sat on the floor after taking a few wipes to clean his hands before pulling both boys onto his lap.

"I miss this. I miss seeing them every day. I never knew this kind of love before them. I mean, I am loved greatly by my family and of course, you already know how much I love Kendra, but this show of love from them is unmatched to anything. I'm meeting with a realtor tomorrow morning before I come see them. Before I fly out tomorrow night, I'm hoping he can find something permanent for me. I don't want to stay in a hotel every time I come here, even if I spend most of my time here. I want to have space for them to spend some nights with me. I don't want to do that in temporary housing."

"I hate that you have to do that. I hate that you have to do this. Life was easier for all of you when they were with Kendra in Hawaii. I think she feels the same way. The stubborn child I raised would never admit that. I'm sorry the engagement didn't work out. I know how much you wanted to make all of you an official family. Even if she doesn't know it, I know you didn't do it simply because you have children together."

"You're right. I did it because I love her. I still love her. I will forever love her. That's separate from loving and wanting my sons. I love us as a package deal. I still don't know what happened. What I do know is, I can't continue to allow her to brow-beat me; to turn a faucet on and off without telling me why. I don't want that kind of confusion around my sons as they are growing up. I'd rather keep the peace by doing things her way, than to keep fighting and being rejected."

"I hear you and I understand. Can I ask a favor?"

Callum nodded.

"Please don't give up on my daughter. I don't think she understands what she has with you. She's got a lot of insecurities. Kendra has never loved like this before. She struggles with how to make sure what you have together will be forever. She has to work through it. I believe she will. If you love her, please don't give up if she comes around and gets herself together. Can you do that?" Melissa asked.

"Ma'am, I would take your daughter back at any time for any reason. It has to be her doing. She has to make the move. I'm fresh out. My begging and pleading days are over. I've proven myself. It's time for her to show and prove. I thought we could mend things if she came back to *Quiet Whisper* for the wedding. She told me she's not coming. I don't know why. I still don't understand. When Kendra figures out what she really wants, I'll be here. We have sons together. I'm not going anywhere."

**

"Callum gone?"

Kendra looked up from her place on the corner of the sofa in her living room. With the boys down for the night, she was having a moment to herself to sulk. She welcomed her father's company.

"Hey, Dad. Yeah, he left about an hour ago."

"Oh good. He had a lot of time with Finn and Liam. I bet they tired themselves out with him. They'll sleep good tonight. Everything is all set out back. I'm loving this new house. It's so perfect."

She looked up at him and put a fake smile on her face.

"I agree."

Kendra answered with no emotion and no expression. It's the same way she was feeling inside. She missed Callum. She just couldn't figure out how to release her insecurities to trust him fully. Her father sat at the other end of the sofa. She felt his eyes on her.

"Why are you doing this to yourself? Why are you doing this to Callum? Why are you doing this to your sons? What's going on with you? We could usually talk about everything. Tell me how I can help."

"You can't. I don't think Callum and I will ever work things out."

"Do you want to? I mean really? He comes here even when he can barely stand because he's so tired, like today. His whole body screamed that he needed rest, yet here he is. He has a place here or is buying a place here so that he can have a place for his

148

sons to have a home just like this one. Every second he gets, that jet heads to Vegas. He's killing himself trying to be all things to everyone, even you. How can you not see how much he loves you?"

"I can't trust him."

"You want him to be perfect. He's not that. He may never be that. None of us are. You're not; I'm not; your mother isn't and he's not. Despite that, he loves you. Why would you choose to do this alone if you don't have to when the man you love wants to make a life with you?"

"Dad, he cheated on me in a way that is hard to forgive and forget. I think he was doing that again in Hawaii."

"You think or you know?" he asked.

Kendra hunched her shoulders. She really didn't know. It was all about what she saw. The appearance was all she needed to see.

"I'm afraid. I love him so much that I'm afraid to have this kind of love for a man that could possibly mess around on me."

"Baby girl, you are giving him a reason to rest in another woman's arms. Is that what you really want? Eventually, he will tire of waiting for you. He will become a man who will walk this life taking care of and bonding with his sons and that's it. You think you hurt now? Imagine loving him and one day he finds another woman to love. He will find another woman worthy of a marriage proposal. The way you love him, I fear what that would do to you. Love isn't perfect. It never will be. What is perfect is you and Callum together. You can make it through anything. Marriage and love aren't easy. It requires consistently working on staying connected. It may mean forgiving mistakes here and there. You love through that and move on together."

"You and mom have a perfect marriage. You don't have doubts."

Her father chuckled and patted his knee.

"Is that what you think? There is a lot about our marriage that you, your brother and sister don't know about because we keep our business between us."

"You would never cheat on mom. You would never make her question her ability to be enough for you."

Silence. Kendra hadn't been looking at her father. When he didn't answer, she turned her eyes his way. He wasn't looking her way either. When he turned around, she saw something in his eyes.

"I would never cheat on your mom...again."

Did she hear him right?

"What? You did?"

"Many years ago when I was an NBA player, yes. I was young, stupid and smelling myself. This was actually after your mother and I were married. Yes, I made a mistake. I got caught up in the fame and spotlight. My popularity as a star center got to my head. Women were coming at me from all angles. I had no excuse for what I did. In my case, I came clean with your mother when I didn't have to. I wanted her to know that I was sorry for what I had done. I knew from the look on her face that I would never, ever do it again. And I didn't. See, as perfect as you always want to see me as in your eyes, and I get that, I am fallible. I was weak. I failed her. I failed you kids. She was home taking care of you. At that time, we didn't have Amelia and TJ. She was pregnant with him. I was a fool. I made sure that from that day on, she would never have a reason to doubt me. Now, she was burning mad at me. That was the end of the season. When I came home, she had already booked a hotel room for me to stay in. She didn't want me in the house."

Kendra was shocked. She couldn't believe what she was hearing.

"What? Mom did that?"

"She sure did. She was serious about me learning the most important lesson. That was, not to play with her ever again. Trust me, I learned it."

"I'm shocked!" she declared.

"For a month, that's where I slept at night. If I wasn't doing promos for the team or other work, I was either here during the day until you and her went to bed or I was in that hotel room lonely as hell. I missed my family. She left me in that misery for a month. At the end of that, we decided to work things out. She needed to work through that. You have to work through this. Don't think you have a lifetime to figure it out. You will look up and another woman will have snatched up that man. He's yours. He always has been and always will be."

"I hear you. Thanks for being honest."

"I'm going to go up and get your mother. I think she was going to finish putting your laundry away. If you need us, let us know. Don't give up the fight. I didn't raise you to be this lump of clay who I see sitting at the end of the sofa. I raised a strong, Black woman who never, ever gives up on what is hers. Think about that."

Her father stood, kissed her on the forehead and took the stairs two at a time, just as Callum had done. She had a lot to think about.

# 13

Callum could hear his phone ringing but being this deep in sleep, he fought waking up to answer it. When it rang a second time, he thought it may be about the boys so he reached for it before it stopped ringing.

"Hello," he said, responding without checking who it was.

"Son. Did I catch you sleeping?" his mother asked.

"Mom? Yeah, I was dead to the world asleep. I haven't gotten more than a few hours' sleep a day for over a week. I knew I was tired, but not this much. What time is it?" he asked.

Opening his eyes, he could see daylight shining through the slits in the blinds at the windows.

"It's almost noon. I can't believe you're still in bed. I'm begging you to get more rest. You can't keep going on like this. It's a death sentence."

"I know but I wanted to spend time with Finn and Liam. You know I had to come. Is everything alright?"

Callum sat up and threw his legs over the side of the bed. He looked at himself. He was still in the clothes he'd had on the day before. After leaving Kendra's house, he'd come right to his hotel room and dropped right down on the bed after taking off his suit jacket and shoes.

"Yes. I wanted you to know that your father and I are here at *Quiet Whisper*. We decided to come in a week ahead of the wedding to get some quiet time. Are you heading this way soon?" she asked.

"I have a stop to make and then, yes, I'll be there. Tellum and I have some things planned for Byrum."

"Wholesome things?" she asked.

"Mom, do you really want to know? I don't think you do," he joked.

"Yes, keep that a mystery please. How are my grandsons? I can't wait to see them in a few days. Is Kendra still coming to the wedding? I know you're not together, but I saw she was still on the invitation list."

"She told me yesterday that she's not going. I don't know why. At this point, I'm going to stop asking why when it comes to anything she is doing. I can't handle the drama. I'm coming back here to get them after the wedding. The boys will be with me in Detroit for about a month. Kendra will come for their birthday party. She may come sooner. No doubt she'll miss them."

"Just as you do when they are with her. Everything is all set for their party. I was hoping to see them while we were here in Hawaii. I guess that's not meant to be. I can't wait to show them off when you get them to Detroit."

"You went overboard on the party, didn't you?"

Callum expected that. He didn't mind. His sons were his miracle babies. Nothing but the best for them."

"All of the family is coming from all over the country. I got the invite list from Kendra's side of the family. I have hotel rooms held for all of them."

"Charge their rooms to me."

"Your father has already said he'll take care of the cost. You're footing the bill for the party. You know, I had a lot of hope for you and Kendra. I know how much you love her. There is a sadness on your face and in your voice. I don't want this anguish for you."

"Initially, I couldn't gather my thoughts for meetings or sleep well without having them under the same roof as me. It's a silence that eats away at me. I don't know what I did. All I can assume is that she is still thinking about what happened with Tessa."

"She's still not telling you what's going on with her?"

"Not a single word."

"Give her time, okay? Nothing is perfect, especially a loving relationship. Listen, I also want to talk to you and your brothers about a birthday party for your father. He hasn't had one in a lot of years. He's coming up on a big number. I'm thinking something black tie in Detroit where most of our really close friends live. With Byrum's wedding coming up, I don't want to focus on anything but him and Keiko right now. I want to be sure a party for your father is on your radar. I haven't mentioned it to Tellum and definitely not Byrum yet. Can you do that in the coming months?"

"Of course. You know we'll be all over that. Keiko's wedding planner has done a wonderful job, according to her and Byrum. We can connect with her after all of the wedding festivities are over."

"I love that idea. Let me just say that I not only want my grandsons there in their little black suits, but I want Kendra to be there. I know you're having problems, but because of the boys, she is and will always be family."

"The boys will absolutely be there. I'm not sure she will be, but I will ask when we get that far along. Or, I will have Cheyenne ask her. They've gotten pretty close."

"I don't care who does it as long as she knows that the invitation is sincere. I wished she was coming here. I was thinking about asking if your father and I could spend a full day with the boys while she was here. I'll reach out about visiting them in Vegas sometimes."

"I'm sure she would love that. She loves you. It's me she can't stand."

"Oh, I doubt that. I've never seen a woman more in love with a man. Give her time, okay?"

"I will. Her mother asked me to do the same thing, to give her time. The two of you must know something I don't know."

"We know what it's like to be in love with a man with every part of our being. Kendra hasn't let go of the ultimate betrayal and is struggling with trusting again. When she's ready, I believe she'll come around. She's supposed to be my daughter-in-law."

"Yes, she is," he said. "That's the realist truth for sure. I'm going to get up and get dressed. I want to see the boys before I fly out. I hadn't planned on sleeping this late. I guess I needed this. I'll see you in a few days?" he asked.

"We'll be here. Kiss the boys for me."

"I will. Thanks, mom."

"Love you, son."

"I love you too."

Callum stood and reached for his phone again after placing it on the nightstand. He sent a quick text to Kendra to make sure she was at the house with the boys. He reminded her that he was only in town for part of the day. She replied right away to let him know that the boys were eating lunch and waiting on him.

There were no personal or intimate pleasantries between them that they once had. It was clearly parent-to-parent chatter. He missed what was more of them. He missed it with everything in him. He had hoped for time to spend with her if she was coming to the wedding. It looks like those hopes were dashed now that she wasn't coming. He was at a point that he didn't know what else to do. He would try and do what his mother and Kendra's mother said do. He would wait.

**

"One day you'll stop fighting the inevitable. If you and Callum were not meant to be, you wouldn't have to fight this hard to resist the love you share. How long are you going to make him pay for that night?"

"Mom, can we not today? I didn't know when you said you were dropping off a package this morning that it was going to come with a speech. I can't today. I have a lot to do. Callum is coming over. I'm going to run a few errands while he hangs here with the boys. Taking them with me is challenging. They hate the stroller and just want to run everywhere. I swear they went from crawling to running," she joked.

"I keep telling you to stop expecting him to be perfect. Your father told me that he told you about his indiscretion years ago. We had struggles, but I loved him enough to not want to end my marriage and ruin our lives. Our love was stronger than that. Maybe, just maybe there were other nights that you don't know about. At this point, that's behind you. Look at all that he has become. Are you telling me that you still see that playboy he once was? You can't believe that. You can't possibly think that he doesn't love you with all of his heart, his soul, his mind and yes, I will say it, even as your mother, his body. I don't profess to know everything but I have loved your father for what seems like my entire life. Is he perfect? No. Are their things about me, him and our marriage that I have shielded my children from? Absolutely. I did that because any wrong does not and will never surpass how much I know he loves me, loves his kids and loves the life we have and will continue to build together. I don't want to see you lose out on the love of your life, the love of a lifetime because you're too stubborn to admit that you have been punishing him for far too long. It happened. He apologized. He didn't dig in with claws when you kept his sons from him until you thought you may lose them. He jumped right in and did all that he was supposed to do. He has gone overboard to keep the peace between you despite you poking the bear over and over so that you were sure he would never forget that slip up."

"What if I think he's done it again?"

"Did he? Are you sure that's what you saw? Did you ask him?"

"No. I couldn't. I didn't want to hear the answer."

"Whew, my child. You can be exhausting with wanting people to read your mind. This is crazy talk. Yes, that's what I'm calling it. I think you young people hold on to things for far too long. He messed up. Maybe your messes in life weren't on that level, but you've had them. What you girls took me through as teenagers tested me every single day. Your brother was a little different. Despite anything, I love every part of you and I always will. Why can't you forgive and forget? When I say forget, I mean that. You say you have forgiven him, but have you really? You can't do that if you have to continue to bring up what he did in order for you to justify not letting your heart love him completely. You know you want to. I see it in you. I saw the fire in your eyes when that young woman walked over to talk to him after you wouldn't give him one freaking dance. I still remember that day. That was the day I knew you were in love with him. This was before my grandsons. I know I keep bringing this up. I don't want to you see you this miserable. You try to hide it. You're not good at that. I hate this for you. I want so much more for you and my grandsons. If the two of you want to walk away from each other and just co-parent, I am in support of that all the way. I wish that was what I saw so that you can stop hurting. You look at him with a love I don't think even compares to what

I feel for your father. Finn and Liam brought you two back into each other's lives. Let the love of them, you and Callum keep you together as a family, if that is truly what you want. If you say, no way in hell do you want to get back with Callum, then I say put your big girl panties on and stop throwing an inward tantrum every time a beautiful woman sees him as a single man on the market for the taking."

"You didn't see him. I know something happened between him and the woman I saw him looking intimately at. He was too close to her to not be up to no good. You didn't see them. I couldn't get out of that pool hall fast enough. I didn't want to relive the Chicago night all over again."

"Either you want him or you need to release him to be with a woman who can appreciate the man he has become. Now, I'm going back home because in a minute, I'm going to cry out of desperation for what I know my child could have; forever happiness; forever love. It's what I want for all of you. You, my child, are closer than your sister and brother to having that, yet you are willing to toss it to the gutter because you haven't learned to look beyond the exterior being imperfect and looking deeper to see what God has created for you. Callum is a man who is walking perfection, not for anyone else, only you. Think about that. And let me just say that the ring Callum showed your father and I was nothing short of magnificent. It sparkled with all of the treasure that a man could offer a woman. It's a shame that this pride you have, that didn't come from me or your father, is leading you astray. You need to go and have fun at Byrum and Keiko's wedding. Your father and I have the boys and they will be fine. At least do that before you leave that beautiful island. Go to that wedding and figure out how to fix things with Callum. The silent treatment doesn't solve anything. That leaves a lot out in the open. You haven't even told him what you saw at the pool hall. I must say, Callum and his brothers sure did create a beautiful resort. I love you, honey. Go and get your life back."

Kendra hugged her mother before she left out. She did something she hadn't done in a long time. She cried for the bitter woman that she allowed herself to become, not just because Callum had cheated on her but because she was embarrassed knowing how people saw her. She hated the thought that women like his ex, Tessa, saw her as a woman who couldn't keep a man like Callum happy to the point that he wouldn't have had to screw her or anyone else. More than all of that, she cried because her mother was right – she forced herself to not forget so that she would never put herself in a position to be hurt like that ever again. The truth was, Callum has done everything except stand on his head in order to win her back. His words of love and devotion didn't fall on deaf ears. He proposed to her and she really turned him down. Her heart was screaming yes at the same time that her lips shouted no.

His sentiments of love fell on a heart that was closed by her own doing. The revelation that there was no man for her but Callum was like a boulder crashing into her. Yes, they'd made love over the past few months that she had been on the island. Is it possible that she didn't see what she thought she saw? She wouldn't know if she didn't talk to him. If her mother could take her father back, and to her, her father was perfect, then she could sit and talk to Callum. There are things she needs to stop doing. One is thinking he could read her mind. Another was doubting his love. There was also her issue with trusting when he says he loves her, that he means it. He has apologized a million times for what he did with Tessa. It was time she let him off the hook for that.

She and Callum were good together; that was true. That

wasn't all that there was between them. It wasn't about the boys either. There was no doubt in this world that he loved Finn and Liam with everything in him. What was also apparent was that, though he loved her physically like a man with a heart filled with desire, passion and thirst, she wasn't sure she was enough for him. Still, perhaps she needed to at least try.

She picked up her phone and called Keiko. She changed her mind. She needed to get her invitation back to the wedding. Packing the boys up to take them to her mother was next on her agenda. Finally, she needed the perfect dress to turn Callum's head and his heart. Enough was enough of making him pay for something he may not have even done.

She picked up her iPad and logged into her airline account and first booked a flight and then added a hotel room for a week. She smiled hoping that she wouldn't need it. If she could get Callum to forgive her for again, not getting it right, it would be well worth losing the money to spend her nights with him, in his arms, in his bed and most importantly, in his heart.

# 14

*Byrum and Keiko's Wedding*

Kendra slipped into her chair next to Cheyenne at the family table at the wedding reception. To say that Keiko was a gorgeous bride would be an understatement. Her radiant smile could be seen from miles away. She was happy that she made it back just in time to see the wedding party dance into the reception all.

Though construction was finally finishing up on the other side of the resort, the main event hall had been completed for months and was the perfect setting for a night of partying. She never knew Hawaii was this beautiful until she arrived with the boys over six months ago. She was happy to be back for the wedding of the year. The second of three Blackstone brothers had taken that leap over the broom. This could have been the second of three if she hadn't been so foolish as to turn down Callum's proposal. Doing so had crushed him. Truth be told, she was crushed, but she hid it well from everyone, especially Callum.

When she watched him having fun, dancing and spinning around the woman whom he escorted down the aisle, her heart hurt, not for him, but for herself. She had seen a brief moment of excitement on Callum's face when he recognized her in the audience once he entered the hall following behind Byrum and Tellum. He and his brother were serving as best men. Her heartbeat sped up when they locked eyes. It slumped again when he looked away. He had remembered they weren't together. At least, that's what the look on his face meant to her. She saw it. She felt it. Still, she was here. She had a purpose to fulfill. She wasn't backing away now.

Seeing Callum happy and having a good time didn't surprise her. It did have her longing for those nights together with him that ended because she was foolish. Though he'd flown to Vegas quite a few times just within the past month, he made it clear that his visits were to see the boys. He had no problem letting her know that he would no longer allow her to walk all over his heart. He finally acknowledged that he was done fighting a losing battle when he didn't know what else he could do to continue the fight, that he hadn't already done. The last time he left, over a week ago, he had kissed the boys, who cried for almost an hour after he left them. They missed him anytime he wasn't around. Now that they were walking, they would race to the door on their tiny little bowlegs anytime they thought he was leaving. Her heart hurt for them. A few times, she saw unshed tears in Callum's eyes. This was her doing. She was hurting them all. Life didn't have to be that way.

She understood that he had a company to run and that took him away often to either Detroit, Hawaii or another location where he was needed. He apologized often for not spending every day and night with the boys. His words pricked her heart when he didn't include her in that. She'd pressed too hard on pushing him away for anything other than the intimacy her body craved and still does, for his loving only. She missed him. She loved him.

"The way you're looking at Callum is speaking volumes."

Kendra smiled but didn't take her eyes off of Callum, even as Cheyenne engaged her.

162

"I love him," she quickly and confidently admitted.

"You're just discovering that? If so, you're the only person who didn't know it."

"I know. I've been so stupid and stubborn. Not anymore. I'm here to set claim on what's mine. I plan to remind him that I am his completely. That is, if he'll still have me."

"What planet have you been living on? Callum is like his brothers, when they love, and I mean really love, they do it forever. You have and always will be the love of his life. You are always his."

"That's what I'm banking on."

Kendra smiled and looked to Keiko who just danced by their table with Byrum twirling her around. Kendra and Keiko winked at each other at the same time. She then looked to Cheyenne with the biggest, brightest smile that she could muster up.

"I saw that. What was that? Are you and Keiko up to something?"

"Absolutely. I'm glad I made it back in time. I have to pump often for my hungry boys. I didn't want to miss their entrance."

"Where are the boys? I didn't see you with them at the wedding."

Kendra shook her head no.

"If they were at that wedding and saw Callum come down that aisle, all hell would break loose. They would have crawled over everyone to get to him. He doesn't know that they're here in Hawaii. I was planning to attend alone and head back to Vegas after a few days. That is, if I were able to work things out with Callum. So much has happened since I decided to come to the wedding. Byrum flew me and my family here together last night. I had made different plans. Then I called Keiko about attending. The next thing I knew, she called a few days later and said Byrum was taking care of us getting to the island. My parents and my sister are here too. They have the boys. I was hesitant about leaving them, so my parents came a few days before they're leaving on a cruise. My sister and I are going to stay a few extra days. Remember I told you about that reality show that I auditioned for? Well, I didn't get a role on the show; I was asked to be the host. The show is being shot right here in Hawaii. I had originally turned it down. I know that Detroit is home for him, but from talks we've had before, he really wants to live, at least a year here. I want to be here with him. I can't deprive him of seeing his sons every day. I can't deprive myself of having the best man as the love of my life."

"Wow! It's all exciting news. Not just about the show but about you coming to the realization that you and Callum are meant for each other. Congratulations on the show. Does Callum know any of this?"

"Not yet. I'll tell him after the festivities are over."

"He'll be excited."

"I know. I'm hoping he'll be excited about more than just that show. I'll share more in a bit. He's so handsome."

Kendra let her eyes follow every move Callum made.

"Yes, he is. There is something about a Blackstone, right?"

"You should know. You locked yours down first."

"So did Keiko."

"Okay, everyone! Let's hear it for our newlyweds and their first dance," Sarai, one of Byrum's executive assistants yelled from the microphone on the stage.

Everyone stood and cheered as Byrum swiftly and softly took Keiko in his arms, first kissing her as if no one else was in the room to the clinking of glasses all over the room, then dancing in circles around her. When he pulled her close, as Sarai continued talking over the noise, everyone stood stunned, unable to move or close their mouths when the mystery celebrity took the stage for the couple's first dance. He bowed in Keiko and Byrum's direction.

"Damn!" Cheyenne yelled. She clapped uncontrollably like everyone else.

"I want to personally introduce all of you to our special guest tonight who will serenade our happy couple. Y'all, let's hear it for R&B icon and legend, *Usher*!"

Kendra could barely contain herself when Usher spun around, took the microphone stand, tilted it almost to the floor, spun himself around again and grabbed the mic before it hit the floor. He was dressed in all black with a red tie to match the colors of the red and black theme of the wedding party. As he sang, all eyes were on Keiko and Byrum. Unlike them, her eyes were on Callum. She wished that he would look her way.

Callum was settled in at the table next to a woman she now knew was one of Keiko's cousins. The woman was stunning with her exotic looks, much like Keiko. Even though she and Callum seemed to have a level of comfort with each other being a part of the wedding party, she wasn't jealous. In the past, any time a beautiful woman sidled up to Callum, jealously would overtake her. Not today. Love was all she saw when she looked at him. Nothing else or no one else mattered. Kendra felt no ill-will toward the woman or Callum. Even if there was more to the woman's intentions with him, which she couldn't blame her or any other woman who flirted with him on the regular, she still only saw a man that was hers; a man she belonged to in every way. That is, if he would give her another chance after millions of attempts on his end that she shot down. She kicked herself throughout the night when she was unable to sleep. Her mind wouldn't let go of the number of times he had begged and pleaded with her. She shook the thoughts off. It was now her time to be the one to beg and plead if that would bring her family back together.

Just when she was about to turn her attention to Usher who was lighting up the stage with his performance, Callum looked her way. She started to smile, but didn't when she saw no emotion on his face. That's how it was when he saw her at in the audience at the wedding. There were times when he would wink at her that she ignored. He would smile to let her know he liked what he saw. He didn't do that either. He just locked eyes and didn't let go. He was hurt. This isn't what she set out to do after he hurt her. She never wanted to see him being wounded in his eyes when he looked in her direction. No more, she thought. There would be no more hurt.

Once Usher was done, Sarai let everyone know that he would be back for more but right now, she said Keiko had an announcement.

This was it she thought. Kendra looked down to make sure her milk wasn't leaking out. That was her main reason for disappearing at the start of the reception so that she could take care of that and not have any issues during the party. Her short red dress and red and gold heels were a statement for sure. It was form fitting just the way that she liked but had strayed away from after her body filled out more after the boys were born. At first, she was uncomfortable with larger breasts and a much more defined and rounded behind. As an athlete, she'd always been in shape. Getting back to that was her goal. Callum continued to encourage her with words that she was perfect as she was but if she wanted to do more, do it for her. He loved all of her new curves. His words fell away because she was behaving like an ass.

"He's mine," she muttered under her breath.

"What?" Cheyenne questioned.

"Callum. He's mine."

"I love this new Kendra. No more doubt in your eyes or in your words. I love it."

"The only person who ever doubted me was me, but not anymore. Thanks to Keiko, everyone will know it too."

"Huh?" Cheyenne questioned.

Kendra then pointed to Keiko.

"I have something extra special on my special day that's not about me but about someone else. All of you know how much I love Byrum. Cheyenne and I share something that not many other people can attest to; there is something amazing about being loved by a Blackstone man."

The crowd cheered. Glasses were raised around the room. Tellum and Byrum both saluted each other; Tellum from his seat at the head table and Byrum from the floor, still holding onto Keiko.

"And you know this!" Byrum said into the mic before Keiko pulled it away, playfully.

"Not that I need a backup singer. I love you, baby. Now, tonight is my night. I can do whatever I want to do. Thankfully, I am not a selfish person, especially when it comes to more love. I've asked our DJ to play a special song for someone special or should I say, two people who are special to us. I am hoping that the desired impact happens just the way the requester is hoping. We all believe in love. I felt like I had to beg, borrow and steal to have the kind of love I have with Byrum. I know what it feels like to love someone so much that you can become scared of what forever could look like. This kind of love is rare. If Byrum and I can help anyone along the way to discover and live in the kind of love we have found with each other, we are onboard. Tonight, Byrum and I are not just celebrating our love. We are sharing our night with love all around us. Without any more words from me, Mike?" Keiko signaled to the DJ.

Keiko and Byrum walked to the edge of the dance floor.

Kendra waited. Her nerves were on a new high when Callum stood and walked toward the exit. She wasn't sure where he was going. Wherever it was, he had the worse timing. She still refused to give up even if she had to follow him out of the door. She prayed he wouldn't leave yet. Now was her time; now was their time. She prayed the song would start before he was gone. Before he reached the door, the song began.

*"You're all I need to get by. You're all I need to get by."*

(Marvin Gaye) *"Like sweet morning dew, I took one look at you and it was plain to see, you were my destiny."*

(Tammi Terrell) *"With arms open wide, I threw away my pride. I'll sacrifice for you, dedicate my life to you."*

Then it happened. Callum stopped moving. He knew. She knew that he knew. It was their song. He played it to her the night he proposed and she said no. It was the song that played on their third date before they went back to her hotel and had the most amazing night of love making. They were young but he made love to her like a pro, like a man who had mastered the art of loving a woman's body. He had been her first; her only.

Kendra stood on legs that were nervously wobbly and moved to the center of the dance floor as the song continued on. She then sang along with it with her eyes locked on the back of Callum's head. He hadn't moved from the door. She exhaled with happiness that he didn't continue through it.

To her delight, Callum looked to Byrum who gave him a thumbs up.

When Callum heard her voice, he turned and saw her standing. She hoped beyond hope that he could see, even from that distance, the full and complete love that she was sending his way. He often said he thirst for her. Today, she was thirsting for him and doing it without any shame. She wanted her man back. She wanted the world to know it.

(Marvin) *"Oh, oh, oh."*

She sang to him.

(Tammi) *"I will go where you lead."*

And then it happened.

Callum smiled and sang with the song.

(Marvin) *"Come on baby!*

(Tammi) *"Always there in time of need."*

(Marvin) *"And when I, lose my will, you'll be there to push me up the hill."*

They then sang together as he made his way to her in the center of the floor. If there was anyone else in the room, she didn't care. She only had eyes for Callum and the fact that he understood the assignment; it was love, forgiveness and the kind of thirst that wasn't a drought but an affirmation of never-ending love from heart to heart.

(Marvin/Tammi together) *"There's no, no looking back for us. We got love sure 'nough, that's enough. You're all, you're all I need to get by."*

Kendra couldn't sing anymore when Callum reached the edge of the dance floor and opened his arms to her. He rocked to the beat of a song that was theirs; it was their love song. She flew to him as fast as her heels would take her. She raced right into his arms, wrapping hers around his neck and crying into the side of his face. He swayed with her, holding her tight against his body. The song continued to play and he continued to sing it to her.

The crowd around them went crazy with catcalls, cheers, claps and everything else to be sure they celebrated more love on the floor that Keiko spoke of. Most people in attendance knew their story. If they didn't, they would before the night was over. This was a romantic scene that she was happy to be a part of.

"I'm sorry, baby," she whispered in his ear, still holding onto him with a death grip. "I'm so sorry. I love you so much. I know I've been crazy. I could chalk it up to post-partum issues, but that's not true. I've been so stupid, so unappreciative of who you are. I forgot what we could be together."

"Baby, it's okay. I love you so much. All you ever had to do was say yes. Whether it was today, next week or next year – you only had to say yes to our love and I would be right here. Our song? You got them to play our song at Byrum and Keiko's wedding," he said as the song came to an end.

"Both of them told me that I better do this. It didn't take a lot of convincing them that I was all over it. Can we talk? I know this is not the best time. The boys and I will be here in Hawaii for a while."

"You will? The boys are here? Where are they?"

Callum looked beyond her, his head turning in all directions.

"At your place with my parents. I didn't think you would mind me using the key you gave me."

"Of course not. That's our place. I didn't change the locks or the code. I hoped beyond all hope that one day you would use it."

"Okay, folks, there is one more song. Callum, Kendra, don't you dare move."

Just then, Kendra placed her hands in Callum's as he took them and held them tight.

"What's going on?" he asked her.

Kendra didn't respond. She wanted to make sure the song that was about to play started first. This was her do or die moment. She was ready.

The opening to, *"Without You"* by Mariah Carey played.

As another one of their favorite songs played, Kendra focused on the man whose eyes were hungrily pouring into hers. With an animalistic thirst searing through her, he relayed his love. His blatant desire caused her body to happily enjoy the sweet feelings his gaze brought about. Love overflowed.

"I can't live if living is without you, Callum. The boys and I can't do anything in this life without you; without us as a family. I love you. If you love me as much as I know you do and you still want me, please ask me again. Please ask me one last time. I promise you won't regret ever taking all of the steps you've been taking to win my heart. It was always with you. It will always be with you; filled with you; surrounded by you. I just want us. I hope you still do. Please, Callum, please ask me one more time," Kendra pleaded.

She reached up to wipe away the flurry of tears that blurred her view of Callum, but he took care of that first. He wiped her tears, kissed her lips as if it would be their last time. She knew it wasn't. This kiss, she knew was the start of a newfound love and understanding between them that said that nothing in this world would tear them apart again.

To her surprise, Callum reached into the inside of his tuxedo jacket and pulled out a platinum ring box.

"Before you ask, I didn't know that you would do this. I didn't even know that you would be here. I was planning to fly to Vegas after the reception to ask you again. You're all I've been thinking about. I wasn't sure if you were still coming because I know you didn't want to leave the boys. I was always coming back for you. I would do it a hundred million times."

Kendra cried harder. She looked around the room at everyone who had the same tears flowing. She saw the same look of love in their eyes at what was happening at this moment.

"Here, I thought I was one-upping you by having Byrum and Keiko help me with the songs. You always know what to say and do. I'm just sorry that I took so long to come to my senses."

As Callum went down on one knee, she thrust her hand out at him so fast that everyone laughed, especially when she started jumping in place knowing what was next. Callum laughed at her. He tried his hardest to hold onto her hand through her bouncing around excitedly.

"Kendra Ciara Grimes, this life isn't worth walking through without you right beside me with every step I take. You really are all I need to get by. This song from the sixties personifies what we have always meant and will always be to each other. You are the strength when I'm torn down but with you, all I see is us going higher and higher together. I love you with every part of me. I want my forever to be with you and only you. Will you do me the honor of being my wife and helping me to become whole again? Without you, I'm a walking zombie. Say you'll be mine?"

"Yes!" she screamed.

Behind them was another scream from the head table – it was Felicia Blackstone. The crowd laughed and cheered with her.

"I knew it! Another Blackstone wedding! She said yes," Felicia yelled.

"It's about time!" David hollered.

As everyone celebrated around them, Callum rose after putting the gigantic diamond on her hand and pulled her in for another salacious kiss. She didn't care who was watching. She kissed her man with a vigor that she knew would get more than a simple rise out of him. Surprising her, Callum picked her up in his arms and headed toward the door.

"Not until after your wedding!" Tellum yelled at them.

Kendra laughed and held on tighter to Callum.

"Before, after, during! It's whenever I want," Callum yelled before taking them outside of the door.

"Put me down," Kendra playfully said.

"Not on your life. Not until I find a bed. Hell!" Callum exclaimed.

"What?"

"Your parents are at my condo with the boys. I can't take you there. The walls aren't sound-proof," he jested.

"You are hilarious. You could slow down, you know."

"No, I can't. I need a bed," he said and looked around the hall as if he was really looking for one to appear right in front of them.

"Callum, if you don't slow down, we'll both be in the floor. You can't carry me like this until you get to a room with a bed. You're carrying me like we are already married and you're going to carry me over the threshold," she laughed and kicked her legs joyfully.

"Baby, you need to worry about whether or not I will wait patiently to get this dress off of you before I get inside of you. Do you know how long it's been? If it wasn't an hour ago, it's been too long."

"You're supposed to be at the reception. You're one of the best men."

"We've already done all the photos. I do believe my brothers, who know what it feels like to love a woman the way I love you, will understand. I did my duty for the day. I have a duty to you and this sexy ass booty at the moment. Then I'll go see my boys. I'm glad they're here. I'm ecstatic that you're here."

"Forever," Kendra added.

"What?" Callum asked, stopping at the event hall main desk. Thankfully, as the owner, she knew that he had access to every

173

room in the place.

"You forgot to add forever. I'm here with you forever and a day. Wherever you are is where the boys and I will be."

"Sounds like the best music to my ears."

Before he could make a comment to the front desk assistant, Callum turned and headed to the elevator.

"Where are you going now?" she asked, holding onto his neck to keep from falling out of his hands.

He then stopped in a long hallway where they were alone.

Callum placed her on her feet and turned to face her.

"Tell me," he said.

Kendra was confused.

"Tell you what?"

"Why? Why did you leave me so abruptly like that? What happened? Did I do something wrong?" he pleaded.

Kendra dropped her head. It was time she told him what she saw and that it doesn't matter now. She can move beyond that night no matter what he may have done.

"I saw you with a woman."

"What? When? What woman?"

Kendra huffed loudly. She was already embarrassed about what she's going to reveal.

"I got jealous with you going out to a club with your brothers. I couldn't let it go. I went there after I left the night club where I went with your cousin and a few of her friends. There were memories of that night I caught you with Tessa."

"Baby, I didn't do anything. I don't understand."

"You were huddled up with a woman off to the side in the hallway that led to the bathrooms. You were leaning over talking directly to her. It looked really intimate. I thought you were cheating on me again. I couldn't handle it. I didn't know what to do. I had to distance myself."

Callum let his head drop. He couldn't believe that this is what tore them apart. Now that he knew, he could explain.

"Kendra, I know her. She's another family member. She's married to one of my cousins. She wanted to ask for money to plan a big birthday party for him. He had gone through stage one cancer and beat it. Their resources were depleted. She didn't know what to do to celebrate him with the lack of funds. She asked for a loan."

Kendra couldn't believe what she was hearing.

"What?" she questioned.

She stood in total disbelief.

"Yes, baby. Her husband was playing pool with Tellum and Byrum. They were keeping him busy so that I could step away with her. He didn't know she was there that night, so she wanted to talk in private. I was asking her what she needed to do. I told her to reach out to my office in the morning and my assistant would give her what she needed. I wanted her to know that it wasn't a loan but a gift because that's what family does. That's what took you away from me? Can you please promise me that you will stop having thoughts and not talking to me about them? The mind can kill the greatest things in life. I don't want that for you, for me or for us. We could have lost each other for good this time. We can't keep doing these up and down moments without talking through them. I know that I have always been the most expressive of the two of us. I'm not trying to change what is natural to who you are. I only want you to trust me. I will never, ever give you a reason to not trust me ever again. I love you; *only* you. I thirst for you; *only* you. I do not and will not have eyes for anyone else. Don't do that to us again."

Kendra started to cry and Callum stopped her with a hot kiss; one that had her ready to tear their clothes off where they stood.

"I will never, ever do that again. I promise, never. So many women make a play for you all the time. I've seen the looks of women tonight."

"That's just it. They are looks. That's it; nothing more. I don't like how men drool over you but I know that if you love me like I love you, I have nothing to worry about. Have the same faith in me that brought you to me in Hawaii when our boys were sick. We good?" he asked.

"We will be once you're naked."

"I got that."

Callum started walking again and stopped.

"What?" she questioned after he kissed her again.

"I almost forgot that I spent the night here last night with the rest of the bridal party. I already have a room and a bed waiting for us."

When the elevator door opened, Callum ushered them inside. He took her hands into his and raised them above her head and back against the mirrored glass of the elevator wall.

"Whew! This view is like watching us from all angles. One day, some couple will test the confines of this elevator and get it in!" she said, loving seeing Callum's reaction to her through all four walls.

"Oh, please. Trust me. Before we open to the public, I plan to christen this elevator with you. We have to be sure if anyone asks about the experience, we'll be able to tell them from our own, first-hand knowledge. Now, back to us. You and this dress? You look amazing in red. You are my gorgeous baby. You're my woman. I am all yours. Thanks for not making me beg and plead for the rest of my life. I was willing to do that."

"I know. I've been acting so crazy when all along, all I've wanted was you. I hate that I made you feel like I didn't love you. I'm glad you didn't give up on us. In the end, neither did I."

"Kendra, I was never going to give up on us. I needed a plan. I hadn't had time to focus on that because of Byrum's wedding. I needed to make sure that this place was ready for that. I thought he would get married in Detroit like Tellum or perhaps at *Silent Whisper*. I'm glad he chose *Quiet Whisper*. The promos from his wedding will have people flocking to this place to have a wedding."

"I've never seen a ceremony so beautiful and romantic. It had all the feels that a romantic at heart like me loves. From the decorations to the bridal party, especially you, it was all so magical. I want to get married here. I can't think of anywhere else for us to seal our love with family and friends."

Callum leaned forward and cut off her words when his lips and tongue found her neck. She sighed with need when he licked, kissed, sucked and then licked again, across every part of her flesh. No doubt, her body will be marked with his love before they leave his room. She moaned her pleasure and hummed out her desire for more of him.

"Baby, I will marry you any and everywhere. How soon?" he asked. "I'm thinking next month."

"Callum Blackstone, I cannot plan a wedding in a month. Besides, we have the boys' birthday party coming up. I know your mother has it covered. I don't want anything to counter the celebration for them."

"Six months?" he asked.

"Okay, I can do six months."

"That will work as long as we can continue with our husband-and-wife activities before during and after that time. Do you know how much torture I've been in wanting you and not having you? Never again."

This time Kendra initiated the scandalous kiss filled with spice on a new level. Making love to his mouth was a great prelude to what she was planning to do to his body when they reached a bed.

Callum, moving his body against hers, grinding into her with a movement that had her ready to seal their love in the elevator, was quickly dashed when the door opened. He took her hand as they pretty much ran down the hall.

"If you don't slow down! It's not like I'm going anywhere ever again. We've got all night or until you're ready to go see the boys."

"All night. We'll figure it out since I know you still pump for them."

"Oh, shoot. My bag is still at the table along with my purse. My pump and everything is in that bag. I'm actually winding that down with their birthday coming up. You swooped me out of there so fast that I forgot about it," she said, giggling when she watched Callum's fingers shake when he attempted to enter the key code into the door.

"See what you do to me? I'm like a drug addict. I can't even control my hands. I'll have someone bring your bag up. While I'm doing that, call your parents and let them know you'll be a little later than planned. Make sure they're good with the boys."

"Then naked?" she asked, kicking off her shoes.

Before he answered, Callum turned her body around and kissed from one shoulder to the other, moving her long hair out of the way. That's when she got her answer. Callum was already unzipping her dress. When it fell away and hit the floor, he whistled when he saw that all she had on underneath was a strapless bra and a thong he knew was there but only because she knew he could see the very thin red strap across her hips.

"Calls later, actually. Naked first."

Kendra helped Callum get his clothes off in record time. He didn't even bother with giving her time to take her thong or her bra off. He first reached between her legs to ready her body for him. She smiled when he discovered that she was more than ready. When his fingers came back dripping with her essence, making either of them wait was not the plan.

"You are always so wet and ready for loving," he uttered against her lips.

"That's because I always want you. All it takes is to have you in my sight."

"Whew, baby! Don't threaten me with a good time on a forever scale!"

Callum picked her up in his arms and slid into her body right in the middle of the floor. He swiftly moved her thong to the side. The feel of him long, thick and hard gave her the delightful pleasure she had also been missing in the time that they were apart.

"Amazing!" Kendra yelled. Her arms went around his neck and their mouths found each other in an intoxicating melding of more than their lips, but also their everlasting love. They were finding each other again. She didn't care they got to forever.

Kendra felt every slow grind into her body. With her legs around his hips, she rode him while he showed her just how much he missed loving her this way. They didn't need a bed. They never have before. When he wanted to love her, he did so wherever they were.

The slippery, loving sounds in the room drove her closer and closer to an orgasm that was sure to shatter her very being.

Callum loved her fully and thoroughly. She loved when he loved her slow but also enjoyed the wild ride when he was in that type of mood.

After a few moments, he moved them to the back of the sofa. Without exiting her body, he sat her behind on top of the back of it. With her behind grasped securely in his hands, he moved in and out of her at a frenzied pace. His torrent growl cascaded across her body as he lightly dug his teeth into her shoulder while his body gave to her and then gave her even more. She rode him. Her eyes captured the strained veins in his neck. Callum was pushing himself to hold out to prolong their pleasure.

Kendra was ready to fly. Nothing ever compared to the feel of how completely Callum's body filled hers. They rocked together. When his hips wound around and around, drawing out her please, Kendra threw her head back and tried hard not to scream and wake up the animals in the ocean. She pumped her hips in tune with his. They loved, and loved and kissed, and then kissed more. Her lips were locked with his until her released hit her. She pulled back with a roar in her throat that couldn't be tamed, much like her body's response to his loving.

"I don't care who hears. Don't you dare hold back. You know I love the sounds you make when I'm making love to you."

Proving his point, Callum drew more out of her by placing his fingers between her legs, rubbing that hard nub that had her head spinning with lightning crashing across her eyes, temporarily blinding her. Her orgasm went on and on, sending her body wildly flailing about.

"Cal!" she yelled again and again as her body rose higher and higher, no control insight.

The moment Callum joined her in ecstasy, she held tighter to his arms to keep from falling. He wasn't just growling, but she heard him roar like a lion in heat through his pleasure. They continued to love each other until their bodies quieted as their orgasms released their mind and bodies to the point that words could be formed once again.

She felt Callum struggle through his when his legs wanted to give out as the remnants of his climax zipped through him, hitting his body with pure satisfaction. She knew the feeling. It's how every encounter with him had her feeling. With his eyes closed, Callum leaned his forehead against hers as he worked to calm his raging heart. She caressed his chest to soothe him. She knew that there was more going on than just his body dealing with a powerful release.

"We made it to this room just in time. I swear, I would have done this in the elevator. I hope you understand the impact you have on me. I needed you so bad. I can't explain it. I'm not home unless I'm inside of you, with you, loving you. Please don't ever leave me again. I don't think I would survive a life without you in it. You and our boys are my life. You are why I live, love and breath. When I say I thirst for you, it's not just a line. Water helps sustain us in life. To me, you are my water. You're also my air. You're my everything. I can't handle being without you. Do you understand that? I need you to do more than understand. I need you to know that my heart beats for you and my boys. That's it. That's the complete story. Without you, it will never beat again. I love you. I love you. I love you. I want you. I need you. I love you," Callum said over and over.

His declaration had tears falling from her eyes. She knew he loved her but she never realized how hurt he has been with her constant rejections. Kendra knew at this very moment that her life would always be with him.

"Callum, baby, look at me," she said taking his face in her hands. When he opened his eyes slowly found hers, nothing would make her ever look away; not ever again. When she saw unshed tears, she knew that this moment was necessary.

"Open," he said and smiled.

"I promise you that I will never, ever, ever leave you again; not for anything. I love you more than this life we're living. Like you, I don't think I could live without you in it. It's not out of need, but out of want; out of desire; out of my undying love for you and for us. We are meant to walk this life together. I know that now. I will never look back on anything that's not going to feed positivity into our love. I'm a little embarrassed that you whisked me out of the reception like that because I'm sure that by now, people know what we're doing. It was all over your face and definitely in your eyes."

"Yeah, you know me. I don't care. They need to be lucky I didn't strip you in the middle of that floor and really give them a show," he joked.

Kendra slapped him good-humoredly on the shoulder.

"I love you loving me, but yeah, I'm going to say no to the audience. This right here though, all day, every day works for me."

"Don't say that too many times. Finn and Liam will end up with a little brother or sister sooner rather than later."

Kendra was about to break out in laughter and then stopped and turned her head sideways at him.

"I know I do not feel you hard inside of me again already! I swear your prowess will have me out here in these Hawaii streets barely able to walk!"

"Speaking of Hawaii, you said something about staying for a while?"

"I'll tell you what. Since you didn't allow me time to stay at the reception to eat and I can't go back now with my hair looking like this, feed me first. After that, we should talk about what forever will look like for us. I'm ready. Are you?" she asked.

Callum moved from inside of her. He picked her up again and walked them toward the bedroom.

"I'm always ready. I'll order us some food. While we're waiting for it, this cowboy could use a ride!"

Kendra leaned her head back and roared with laughter. This

was her man; this was the man whom she would never deny anything; especially not a ride that would benefit them both. She reached around and swatted his naked behind as they walked.

# 15

*Three Years Later*

Felicia Blackstone had once wished that at least one of her sons would get married and give her some grandbabies. As she looked out across the large backyard of her home at how her family has grown over the past few years, she got her prayers answered and then some.

The yard was decorated for a family cookout along with lots of activities for the kids. This day had been planned for months. With busy sons and their blooming families and businesses, she had to put her foot down about everybody taking a break to come together to celebrate and be thankful for all that they had.

"Happy?"

Felicia leaned her head back in her patio lounge chair, admiring the view from under the covered deck. The moment her husband walked up, she knew what was next. She puckered her lips and waited the few seconds for him to lean down to connect their lips.

"Happy beyond my dreams. Look at this view," she said, pointing to her sons and their families before pointing to his chair right next to her. Dennis sat down after handing her a cold class of strawberry lemonade, her favorite drink.

"Today has been a perfect day. The sun is shining and we have our family all in Detroit at the same time. You always work your magic when it comes to them."

"Hmph. They know not to play with me. I don't ask for much but once a year, I expect them to coordinate their schedules and come home from wherever they are. I don't care what business is happening. There is nothing more important than family. Look at how happy in love they are. To think, I was concerned that none of them would ever give up their wild boy ways."

"Hey, if I could do it and snag the perfect woman, I had hopes that my sons would too. Each of them chose well. That's why they are so happy. There is nothing greater in life and in love than finding the perfect woman and having a bunch of babies."

"Very true. What I didn't expect was to have all three of my daughters-in-law pregnant at the same time. Tellum and Cheyenne, with two kids already, are having a son in three months. Then we have Byrum and Keiko who I wasn't sure they were going to start a family anytime soon. Looks like they'll be parents to not only Tru, but he'll have a baby brother in a month. Byrum needs to get a pillow to put under her feet. She looks uncomfortable."

Felicia started to get up and her husband stopped her when he pointed.

"Look. Your son knows. He's heading her way with a pillow. We taught them right. They take great care of their women while also running a multi-million-dollar business. They have more wealth than any of us could have ever dreamed. I'm glad to see that though business is important, they understand the importance of the life they live with their wives and babies," Dennis said.

"Speaking of babies, I really thought that Finn and Liam, at almost four would have been enough for Callum and Kendra, but I guess not. I think she said she's four months along."

"Is there only one baby this time?" Dennis quipped.

"Only one. You know those little boys give them a run for their money. They are as rambunctious as our boys were at that age. Speaking of boys," Dennis said and stood.

He got up just in time to catch Finn who was running in their direction at top speed. He ran right into Dennis' arms.

"Poppy, can we have ice cream? I'm hot," Finn said. Dennis sat down with him on his lap.

"Did you ask your mommy or daddy? What did they say?" Felicia asked reaching over to fix Finn's shirt which was twisted around.

"Mommy said to ask Poppy to get it."

"Okay. Then I guess that means Poppy is on the job. Sit here with Granny and I'll get it."

"I love you, Granny," Finn said, moving to sit on her lap.

"I love you, too, and more than what?" she asked before kissing his cheek.

"More than all the ice cream in the world," he properly said.

"Mom, I got him," Callum walked over and said.

"No worries. He's fine."

"Can I get you anything else to eat? The chef is finished cooking. He made lots of leftovers for us all to take home."

"I'm good for now, though he should leave some of the hotdogs out. I will want a few more. Did everyone get enough to eat?"

"Yes. We ate up some food. Thanks for planning this. It will be an every year event, right?" he asked.

"Absolutely. It doesn't have to be here. If one of you want to host it, I'm fine with that. We can do it here in Detroit, at one of your houses or away somewhere."

"Tellum and I were just talking about an idea."

"We were?" Tellum asked walking up behind Callum.

"Yeah. I told you Byrum said that we should head to the family compound in Hawaii next year. We have so much family there that we only get to see in the few short trips we take to check on the resort. You spend time there, mom, because of the foundation, but not all of us at the same time like today."

"Oh, yeah, we did talk about that."

"Well, I'm assuming we'll have to wait a bit for that with all of these babies. We won't know who can fly and who can't."

"Says the woman who couldn't wait to get a football team number of grandbabies. Ask and you shall receive," Tellum kidded.

"And we love every single one of them; even the ones on the way," Dennis said joining them with ice cream in hand just as Byrum walked up.

"Yes, we do," Felicia said.

"I'm going to take Finn with me and hand out ice cream," Dennis said leaving all three sons with her.

"You all make this old lady very proud. You're wonderful businessmen, great men and amazing husbands and fathers. I can't ask for anything more from any of you. You have always been my world. Now you know what I meant when I said, many years ago, that when you slowed down long enough from being bachelors, the right women would come your way. Look at each of you now. Lovely wives and beautiful children. Everyone is happy and healthy. No one would ever think that the twins had medical problems when they were born. They love running everywhere. Tru has fit right in as if he was always a part of this family. It's good that they can all grow up together and do it right here in Detroit. I didn't know what kind of plans each of you had for where you would call homebase for your families."

"Mom. You thought that we would move away and rob you and dad of precious time with us and your grandbabies? No way.

My new house is just about ready. Cheyenne and I are finally moving out of the two-floor loft condo and into a house with a big back yard for the kids to play in," Tellum said.

"Yeah, and Keiko and I moved into our new home two months ago with the same idea in mind – more space for the kids to play," Byrum said.

"I already had my house here, which we all know. All Kendra had to do was expand after we purchased the house next door to us, giving us eight square feet."

"Damn, bro. How many more kids are you planning to have to fill up all of that space? I have to say, I love the pool. That's the one amenity I had to expand on at our house because Tru will one day be an Olympic swimmer. A large pool was a must," Byrum added.

"This life is good, mom. Building those romantic resorts taught us a lot about the value of being in love and staying in love. It was time to put our wild ways to rest, other than when it comes to our wives," Tellum said.

"TMIS," Felicia said. "Way too much information sharing, but I get it."

"Yeah, you and Pop were perfect examples. I think my wife is signaling for me," Callum said before running off.

"Callum is right, mom. Thanks to you and Pop for being what we needed to see, feel and hear when it came to love," Byrum said before he headed off when Tru yelled if he could finally get in the pool.

"You started this love train, Tellum. I'm happy that your brothers could see through how you loved Cheyenne, that there was nothing bad about giving your heart to a woman and making life count with that one."

"No, mom. You and Pop started this by what we see in the two of you every day. I didn't know I could be this happy. I know

Byrum and Callum feel the same way. Looks like the baby is woke and it looks like, looking for me. Let me go get her and get her changed and cut up a burger for her to eat."

Felicia watched her sons interact with their families and knew that the most important part of family is having strong models of love for the offspring who would then bare amazing fruit. Her sons were well on their way.

# Epilogue

*One year later at Quiet Whisper*

Callum walked hand-in-hand with Kendra as they strolled along the beach kicking up water and sand. They were back to what they considered the most romantic place in the world. It was where their love was rekindled and solidified. It was only natural that they took time away from everything and everybody to focus on them.

"Are you ready to be a mommy again?" he asked her as they walked.

"I wasn't sure how I would feel about another baby after the twins and then our baby girl, Ariah. I think I was more worried that something may be wrong. That thought kept me from being as excited as I really wanted to be."

"No worries though, right? I mean, we went to see some of the best Obstetrics and Pediatric doctors, along with heart specialist in the country when they convened at Johns Hopkins Hospital in Baltimore just for us. They did it for baby number three and they did for this one too. Not one of them seemed concerned. All of the tests they ran showed that this little girl does not show the signs that Finn and Liam showed. We worried about Ariah and she was fine too. Though, I was shocked to be pregnant again so soon after having her, I'm just as happy as I was with the other three."

"I told you that you have the worse pull-out game ever!" Kendra kidded.

"As long as you have no problem having my pretty little babies, I have no problem making them with you. Even with their health issues, they are five and thriving now. No worries."

Kendra looked over at him and then looked away quickly.

"I should have done a better job with having them monitored when I was pregnant. I didn't know."

"Baby, no, don't do that. We have two completely healthy, happy and busy little boys. Even though they are doing well, we get them checked out by the best, often. I had the same heart problems that they had and look at me. I can keep up with my wife's sexual desires and still make it through the day. Our boys will be fine and so will our daughters. In four more months, she'll join our family and we're ecstatic about that. I don't want you to worry. We've got this. I'm glad we came here for some down time before the baby comes," Callum explained.

"I talked to my mom last night. My sister is spending the week with her while my dad's team is on the road. You know how they love when their aunt Amelia spoils them."

"That they do. This time with you is for us to not worry about anything. I only want to love on you and you on me. Most of all, quiet time with no distractions. I have some massages planned for us at the resort. We'll have more room service than two people can stand. I bought all of that bubbly, flower smelling bath stuff that you like. I'm going to focus on giving you my perfect foot and back rubs. Tell me what you need."

Kendra stopped walking and turned to him.

"You. All I want and need while we are here is you. Thanks for this time. I know you've been busy with plans for two new resorts. I know the importance of getting those off the ground because *Secret Whisper*, *Silent Whisper* and *Quiet Whisper* are all booked up well over a year in advance."

"Yes, baby. Booked up and busy."

"What about you? Are you happy?" Kendra asked.

"Happier than any man walking this earth. I have you, my wife, thanks to the biggest and best wedding of the year a few years ago. And you thought you couldn't do it. It's a good thing you did. I don't know how much longer I would have been able to wait before making another baby."

"I can't wait until she's here to make us a family of six. I love this resort. I've been to all three and even though I could be biased, I do believe *Quiet Whisper* is the best. I say that because at any time, we can come alone, like now, or we can bring our kids and make it a family getaway. Promise me that you will always thirst for me. If you find that you don't, tell me."

"Baby, I will always want you. I will always thirst for you. I will forever be your everything. I sacrificed this life with you once, before I even knew it was possible. There is no other life I would rather have than what I have with and our children. Now, no more talk of uncertainty. One thing you can count on is your man is always thirsty! Can we go back to our suite? I'd like to make sweet love to my wife."

# *Upcoming Novels*

Get ready for a new series based out of Las Vegas, also known as *Sin City*. First up in the four-book series, *House of Cards*, will be *Ace of Spades*.

Asia "Ace" Wingate is being given the chance of a lifetime to go from barely making it, to living a lavish life in the city that showed her that using what she has to get what she wants became her mantra. When she meets Dakota Croft, a Las Vegas "Gigolo", she gets more than she bargained for. Just when she thinks she's playing him like a masterful card shark, she discovers that she's the one with her cards stacked on the table and Dakota is the man who has a plan to topple it over until it comes falling down.

One steamy night after another is the name of Ace's game to get to what she wants; ten million dollars. Dakota is playing a different game. His is called, win, never lose and only withdraw when she's satisfied because he's playing for keeps.

Come with Ace on a rollercoaster ride in a game of money, power and respect to see if the woman who usually wins can outsmart the one man she underestimated.

*Book 1, Ace of Spades*, in the *House of Cards* series, is available for preorder at www.amazon.com/dp/B0DSZGZYDG

Following, *Ace of Spades*, get ready for the stories of her siblings in, *Jack of Hearts, Queen of Diamonds* and *King of Clubs*.

Sin City will never be the same again with the Wingates on a mission to make Las Vegas bow down and salute them as they make it to the top by any sexy means possible!

### *Never Can Say Goodbye*

Book editor, Taryn Novack turned the idea of falling at someone's feet into her personal nightmare. She'd met attorney, Adrian Jarreau a few times in her aunt's New York Apartment building and found the man irresistible. His hard body wasn't the only 'hard' part of him that she was able to lay her eyes on when she tripped and fell at his feet with him dressed only in a towel wrapped around his hips and nothing else. She could have gotten away with her dignity in place until she decided to look up from his feet to...

Adrian knew that Taryn had been avoiding him since that fateful day that he couldn't remove her and his most embarrassing moment. With her being back in New York after the passing of her aunt, they are thrusts together in more ways than one. Moment gone, their whirlwind affair is about to come to an end and she's set to return to Paris. Can she say goodbye and walk away from him without looking back or ever looking up again?

Secure your copy of "Never Can Say Goodbye" on Kindle Unlimited and paperback on May 31, 2025.

# *Recently Released Novels*

**Hunger for You**, Book 1 of the *Island Embers* series

Tellum Blackstone was entranced the moment his eyes landed on Cheyenne Reddick and her magnetic beauty. In her eyes, arms, and heart, he thought he'd found forever. A rift between their fathers had him questioning what kind of real love could be torn apart with a line drawn in the sand.

Cheyenne never thought that she would meet the perfect man until she did in Tellum. He exuded the kind of charm, kindness, and simmering heat that had her mind, body, and soul sizzling like no man had ever done before. To her dismay, a ticking time bomb of epic proportion, in the form of her father, brought about an ultimatum for her to choose a man she loves from a family he detests or lose his love and support forever.

At *Secret Whisper*, a romantic island resort owned by Tellum, Cheyenne finds that his passion-infused hunger for her easily penetrated her paper-thin resistance. Their desire for each other reignited an insatiable appetite that no woman in her right mind could fight.

Tellum put his all into their red-hot kisses and explosive days and nights of seduction. He needed to find a way to overshadow the risk they were taking in discovering if their love was worth fighting for.

Catch up on book 1, Hunger for You
www.amazon.com/dp/B0CQZG6CXK

***Desire for You***, Book 2 of the *Island Embers* series

Byrum Blackstone is considered the one Blackstone brother who could not be tamed by any woman, no matter how salaciously desirable she is. That is, until he finds himself vulnerable to the one woman he should stay far away from; his executive assistant, Keiko Lee.

In the midst of fighting for her freedom and for custody of her son, Keiko vows to never trust another man with her heart. What she didn't expect was for her boss to offer her wicked, blood pressure spiking, hotter than she's ever known before nights of passion that stir her body and her heart back to life.

Neither Byrum nor Keiko are willing to admit their true feelings as the bigger problem of losing their careers overshadows how bittersweet newfound love could be not just in the present, but in the foreseeable future.

Now available

https://www.amazon.com/dp/B0DL4MKVRT

Get all eight books in the *Brothers of Chi-Town* series

## *I Can't Let Go, Book 1*

Carter Garrison vowed to love, honor and cherish his wife, Sienna, forsaking all others, something he forgot to do during a weekend of fun, bad company and poor judgement. Sienna Garrison never dreamed her college sweetheart, Carter, whom she pledged her life to, would break her heart and when he did, she moved out and moved on - or tried to. What better occasion is there than a friend's wedding to stir up old feelings and memories of love, intense passion and nights of sensual titillation. Gazes from across a room after almost two years apart revealed depths of love that had never died. Seeing Sienna again reminded Carter of what he'd lost and he vowed to never let go by doing whatever he could to get his wife back even if it included begging and pleading. Is Sienna ready to forgive and take a chance on life again with the only man she'd ever really loved? When Carter brings on the charm and turns up the heat, no woman is immune, especially Sienna.

## *Swagger and Baggage, Book 2*

It's not a coincidence that casino owner, Torrence Allen, ran into his college sweetheart, Reese Michaels again; it's fate. As his memories unfold, he had tried everything to keep her in his life and his bed back then and failed at both. She wasn't ready for him then, but he hopes she is ready for him now.

Reese Michaels never thought she'd see Torrence again. Their split in college was dramatic and hurtful and still, no man had been able to win her heart. She considered herself the permanent third wheel to friends who had found love and marriage. Their whirlwind affair, quickly turned into love just as it suddenly crashed and burned when a woman shows up to claim Torrence as hers. When it's also revealed that this woman isn't the only 'other woman', Reese finds herself left with a broken heart, shattered love, and dreams of forever beyond her reach. How did she not know about the other part of Torrence's active and amorous life?

Torrence isn't ready to give up on having Reese in his life after his deceit. He finds himself in the fight of his life to finally have the love and commitment he wanted only with her. His swagger had always won women over, but it's his baggage that's causing his life to spiral out of control and he could once again find himself without the woman he has always loved.

*Claiming His Child, Book 3*

Business magnate Dexter Patterson refused to let anything keep him from checking off all of the boxes equating to achievement in life to prove that though he came from a rough childhood on the south side of Chicago, he still thrived and became a success. Looking around at those closest to him, Dexter found that he was still missing something...Love.

When aspiring model, Alyssa Kincaid met Dexter, she couldn't get enough of his sexual magnetism, fiery nights of passion, and secret rendezvous. She thought they were headed toward forever when a surprising call from him ended what they had causing her to leave Chicago, taking with her a secret.

Dexter thought that no woman could ever tame him, not even Alyssa who entranced him with her sexy body, smoky, sultry voice and untamed desire. Too little, too late, he realized he'd made a mistake by walking away and then she was gone. Time and distance didn't diminish the chemistry between them and the child Alyssa carried and never told him about had him in the fight of his life to win back her heart and the chance to have the family he'd always wanted.

Will Alyssa continue to curse kismet when Dexter suddenly reappears in her life or will she believe that his yearning for her isn't just because of their child, but because when she left Chicago, she took his heart with her?

*Always Bet on Black, Book 4*

Sexy, debonair, Delvin "DJ" "Black" Michaels, left Chicago as a man in search of a better life than the one he had where everyone knew him as "Black". He met a woman, fell in love, and then she turned out to be someone he didn't really know when her scandalous life ruined his career.

Avalon Hart had lived her life on the edge, making do the best way she knew how even if it meant scheming men out of their hard-earned money. She learned how to survive from the streets and she was a woman who had a way with men that got her whatever she wanted, that was until she encountered DJ Michaels in Chicago, a man from her past whom she had once easily swayed to her desires. She realized early that the man she encountered in New York had grown immune to her tricks, even the ones she learned how to do in bed that he loved so much.

DJ and Avalon are on a roller coaster ride to love and neither knew it. He had a lot to lose if he let Avalon get too close to him again. This time, whatever she was plotting, he was ready to take her down, even if it meant losing his heart in the process. He was betting on "Black" for the win, but so was Avalon, in her own way. There was no telling who would end up on top, but one thing was for sure – the road to getting there was going to be filled with hot, sexy fun, a pair of handcuffs and a whole lot of sensuality that neither could resist!

*It Takes Two to Tangle, Book 5*

Councilman Tucker Glass, a native of Chicago, has set his eyes on the biggest prize, that of Mayor of the city he has loved all of his life. At thirty-nine, his career spans back many years as a City Council member and then most recently, as City Council President. His resume reads like a ratings-topper novel full of accomplishments that make him more than qualified for the job, but what he wants to avoid is the drama that could block his path to the mayor's mansion. He's always been a strait-laced politician, but his personal life could spawn a real-life reality show complete with hair pulling, tongue-lashing and accusatory finger pointing which would all occur in the first episode. Tucker wasn't expecting his past to come back to haunt him just as he'd found the woman who was making his life complete. He would do anything to keep her in his life, but is he willing to give up his run for the mayor's office to keep that love in-tact? Nichelle Michaels didn't know that love could be so right until she met and fell in love with Tucker Glass, a man fourteen years older and wiser than her, but who showed her how a man should treat a woman, and that's after she spent the past year testing the water between how a man loves and how a woman loves. Now that she knows what she wants, a woman from Tucker's past could ruin her perfect love. Tucker and Nichelle are in love, but is he willing to risk his chance at being Mayor because his ex-wife, or the woman he thought was his ex-wife, wants to now be First Lady of Chicago? Was he really ready to tangle with a woman who specialized in drama every day on television as the star on the nation's number one reality show? Tucker may be ready for Chicago, but is Chicago ready for the drama that comes along with the popular politician?

*Crashing Into Love, Book 6*

His name is Joseph Kincaid and while most call him Joey, the women of Chicago call him a variety of sexy epithets that are too salacious to utter in public. He's a professional wrestler who is unmatched in the ring, untamed in his response to confrontation and unleashed when it comes to his bedroom proclivities, bringing women pleasure beyond their amorous fantasies. For the second time in her life, Marlow Warren was responsible for an accident that altered someone's life. The first time, she ran to avoid bringing disgrace to her family while hiding from her past, but this time, she's all about making amends to the man whose life she ruined. Everything changed when Joey and Marlow's lives collided. It wasn't all bad. Hurt, anger and unending apologies turned into lust, desire and unbridled cravings, something neither of them could fight. When Marlow's past arrives in a threatening way, Joey knew he would risk his life to protect her because he was now fighting for more than a future back in the ring; he was ready to fight for love.

Carlos Kincaid is an irresistible, rugged loner who is the epitome of that good guy who finishes last when it comes to women. His life is finally on track when Everly Robinson, his Achilles' heel returns to Chicago to turn his world upside down. She stirs up memories of their inexhaustible, hot, steamy, lust-filled nights that he thought were long gone.

Everly chose the wrong man one time too many in her life. She finds herself on the run from two dangerous men, one who conned her into leaving the only love she's ever known and the other whom she calls her father. In desperate need of help, she escaped a mental and physical prison to go in search of the one man she trusts and has always loved.

Carlos is frustrated that old feelings could lead him back into the arms of the woman he needed to hate in order to move on. He couldn't tell if her story was filled with lies or truths. Against his better judgement, he's ready to risk his heart and his life for a woman who once betrayed him and his love.

Tightly wound casino owner, Horace Grant didn't know what family meant until the day his best friend Torrence called him brother. Finding his footing in life in Las Vegas, he put the word 'sin' in "Sin City" with the wicked relationships with women that came with having money and power. Soon, that was no longer enough for him. Making a move to Chicago, his newfound friends showed him what was missing from his life; real, true love.

Angel Reagan has been a lost soul for most of her adult life. For years, she'd been running away from facing the bleak reality of life without her son who died and a family who made her feel nothing but shame. Having unconditional love was never something in her grasp until she met Horace, a man who cared for her like no other.

Horace and Angel are two broken souls who discover that life may not come at them straight with no chasers, but love can break through even the smallest crack in concrete.

Can Horace, who knows everything about gambling, trust his next gamble on his heart?

## *The Brothers of Chi-Town Series*
## 8-Book Series

I Can't Let Go
Swagger and Baggage
Claiming His Child
Always Bet on Black
It Takes Two to Tangle
Crashing into Love
Leaks, Lies, Lust and Love
Love's Gamble


## *The Sullivans of Montana*
## Complete 5-book series

Home for Thanksgiving
The Way You Love Me
On the Right Track
Three's a Crowd
The Law of Love

**WWW.CHERYLBARTON.NET**

# Also by Cheryl Barton

www.cherylbarton.net
*\*Upcoming Novels*

## Romance

### Sister Act
An Unexpected Destiny
For You I Will
More Than Friends

### Bachelor Series
Bachelor Not for Sale
A Designed Affair
A Perfect Combination
Love at Last

### A Lovers' Heart Series
Heartthrob
Heartbeat
Heartbreaker

### Island Embers
Hunger for You
Desire for You
Thirst for You

### Amorous Occupations
The Artist
The Bookkeeper
The Chef
The Dancer
The Electrician

## Stand Alone Romance

Snowbound
Cupid's Arrow
One Wish
His Halloween Promise
Holly for Christmas
A Better Man
Bossy
Un-Break My Heart
Love on Top
Take a Knee
Love at First Sight
My First Love
Black Love
A Younger Man
One Moment in Time
The Lake House
True Lies or True Love
When I Think of You
And Then There Was You
Baby, Come Back
Unforgettable
The Power of Seduction
Seize the Moment
A Christmas Wish
It Should Have Been You
The Christmas Layover
The Sweetest Revenge
The Sweetest Temptation
The Diner
Dashing Through the Snow
A Trick and a Treat
Love Therapy
Mister Christmas
*Never Can Say Goodbye**
*Against All Odds**

# Upcoming Urban Drama

*Amerikka: Justice or Revenge*
*Seven Days: Straight Outta Baltimore*

# About the Author

Cheryl Barton lives in Maryland and in her spare time she loves to read espionage, crime and romance novels, cook, watch Sci-fi movies, spend time with family and friends and enjoy Maryland steamed crabs.

Cheryl is the author of over forty romance novels, four inspirational novels and is proud of six book compilation projects with several other incredible women.

Cheryl was a 2019 Finalist for the Emma Award given by Romance Slam Jam and a 2018 Finalist for the Literary Trailblazer of the Year award by the Indie Author Legacy Award. Cheryl is a member of Maryland Romance Writers at https://marylandromancewriters.com/our-members/member/244/

Cheryl's books are available on her website as well as www.bn.com, www.amazon.com and www.kobo.com

## Connect with Cheryl Barton
Author Cheryl Barton website
www.cherylbarton.net
Amazon Author Page
www.amazon.com/author/cherylbarton
Instagram: @cherylbartonauthor
Facebook: @authorcherylbarton
Threads: @cherylbartonbooks@threads.net